A Dreamer's Revenge

A Dream Catchers Novel

Shawn Dalton-Smith

Indulge a Dream Publishing

Copyright © 2023 by Shawn Dalton-Smith

All rights reserved.

No part of this publication may be reproduced, distributed, or transmitted in any form or by any means, including photocopying, recording, or other electronic or mechanical methods, without the prior written permission of the publisher, except as permitted by U.S. copyright law.

The story, all names, characters, and incidents portrayed in this production are fictitious. No identification with actual persons (living or deceased), places, buildings, and products is intended or should be inferred.

Book Cover by Maria Spada

ACKNOWLEDGEMENTS

Want to send a special shout-out to Bridgette Hyche, Maria Manzo, and Alicia Alford. Thank you for your patience while waiting for this book to be born. And last but never least, my BFF's since sixth grade, Rita Williams and Denneane Hardin. Love you ladies. Ya'll rock!

To Sheldon, my ride-or die guy. Thank you for your support and encouragement when I wanted to quit. I love you!

CHAPTER 1

Astrid busied herself folding napkins and fussing with place settings in the corner of her sushi restaurant, trying not to stare at the man lounging at his table across from her.

He'd been in the night before, and held her gaze every time she dared to look his way. His mocking smile let her know he didn't mind her surveillance, and he wanted her to know he was taking his turn surveying her.

Clean shaven, bald, and skin the color of honey. His mouth held a bit of tension, adding another level to his 'do me baby' smoldering look. The black polo shirt he wore accentuated his muscled chest, without being stretched tight.

Casey sidled up beside Astrid whispering, "You wanted to fill in for Gary, and that's his table." She moved to block Astrid's view. "Hottie sure ain't shy about letting you know what's up. Why don't you go on over there and offer that fine wine a sampler's platter?"

"Hm, I've always wondered if hiring a friend was a good idea." Astrid rolled her eyes. "I don't mix business with pleasure. Especially since I own the place."

"Well, maybe you should. You've been a real grouch lately. Someone needs to clear the cobwebs."

"You know that's not my style, girl. Now go on and do your job." Astrid shooed Casey from the table. "Let me worry about my cobwebs."

"Go get yours." Casey breezed by Astrid, then leaned in. "I want details."

Astrid smirked. "As always."

Strolling to the stranger's table, she flashed her most welcoming smile. "Hi there, welcome back." When he didn't respond, she continued. "Have you decided on what you'd like, or do you need more time?"

"I know what I want."

Those few words, deep and pleasant, carried a bit of an edge. His dark brown, sexy eyes bore a dangerous gleam, reminding her of something. Something she couldn't quite put her finger on.

"I'll have the house sashimi platter. Do you use fresh ginger?"

A smile teased the corners of Astrids lips. Customers often complimented the food, but none ever noticed the ginger. "Yes. It's locally sourced and pickled right here in the restaurant."

"I thought so." His grin widened. "I love it. Could you add a little extra to my order?"

There it was again. There was something familiar about his smile. "No problem." Turning to leave, she paused when he picked up his water glass.

The large black stone in the middle of his gold ring twinkled.

Breathe. Just breathe. "Excuse me, mister..."

"Cyrus. No mister, just Cyrus."

"Cyrus. That's a beautiful ring you're wearing. Very unusual." Keeping her tone causal, she leaned forward for a closer look. "What kind of stone is that?"

No mistake. It was a Catcher's ring.

The Legacy had sworn to let her leave the Dreamers with no strings. But, without them watching her back, she was a sitting duck for the Catchers.

She'd thought she'd been careful. Made sure to keep herself isolated in her dream state. There was no way the Catcher's should have been able to find her.

Holding his hand up so she could study the jewel closer, he slid her a sidelong glance. "It's a family heirloom." His words were slow and careful. "Not really the kind of thing I normally wear. It's handed down to the first-born males in my family, from my great, great, grandfather down to me." He studied Astrid's face as if waiting for a reaction.

Astrid nodded and forced a smile, despite her pounding heart. "What a lovely tradition. I love things like that." She widened her smile. "Your order will be right out."

She turned from the table, hoping the beads of sweat forming on her upper lip would go unnoticed. She forced herself to walk, instead of run, to her office in the back of the restaurant.

Casey rushed in behind her and closed the door. "Are you okay? You look like you've seen a ghost."

"I'm not feeling well." Astrid tried to steady her voice. "He wants the sashimi platter. And make sure he gets a double order of ginger."

"Er, okay." Casey arched a brow. "Who the hell eats double ginger?"

"My thoughts exactly." Faking a chuckle, she patted Casey's shoulder with mock sympathy, and assumed a playful tone. "Sorry honey, I'm afraid Mr. Sexy Pants is just going to have to wait."

Casey arched a brow and pursed her lips. "Don't worry about a thing." Her forehead creased in concern. "I'll call Laura and ask her to cover. You go home and get some rest."

"Thanks." Astrid slung her apron over the back of the chair and grabbed her purse out of her desk drawer. Keeping her head down, she rushed through the kitchen and out the back door.

What the hell am I going to do? She knew a Catcher's ring when she saw one. Maybe it was a coincidence. No one knew she was a Dreamer. Not even Casey. She'd worked hard to leave that part of her life behind. But what were the chances that a Catcher just happened to be in her restaurant?

Checking the back seat of her car before getting in was a habit she'd had for years, and she breathed a sigh of relief each time she saw the empty space.

"Calm down, Astrid," she muttered to herself, getting in. "Just calm down." She started her car and took several deep breaths, attempting to slow her breathing.

Fighting the urge to speed home, she frequently checked her rear, and side mirrors to make sure she wasn't being followed.

Once home, she closed her garage door as soon as the tail end of her car cleared and slumped in her seat. She grabbed her phone from the center console and checked her interior cameras, making sure none of the motion detectors were interrupted. Nothing.

She crossed the threshold to her large kitchen. It was what sold her on the house. She loved to cook, and this house had more than enough counter space.

Her friends thought it amusing that she enjoyed cooking American cuisine, but owned two sushi restaurants. 'Roll With It' was her favorite of the two. It was smaller, laid back, and catered to a younger crowd. 'The Silver Lotus' was a lot more formal and elegant. She'd seen countless business meetings and romantic dates in the six years it'd been open.

Placing her purse on the counter, she went to peer out the front windows to ensure no one followed her.

Shaking her head at her own paranoia, she went out to check her mailbox, pausing in the driveway to take advantage of the lingering daylight.

She adored Atlanta summers. It didn't get dark until after nine. Inhaling the wild honeysuckle scented air from the bush next to her house, she pulled out the small stack of envelopes and walked back inside.

Plopping down on her couch, she thumbed through her mail.

She paused at the creak of the floorboard behind her. It had to be her imagination. No way could anyone get into her house while she was at the mailbox. They would have had to pass her.

The deafening silence always made her aware of every sound, and even the smallest noise from her settling house would rattle her nerves. She gave herself a mental shake and continued with her mail.

Another creak, this one louder, made the prickly hairs on the back of her neck stand on end. She slowly placed the envelopes on the table, and stood, a chill slithering down her spine.

"Dreamer." The deep, familiar voice drew the word out.

A hand clamped over her mouth, and cold steel touched her neck. "Don't worry Dreamer, I don't want to kill you. I need you." Pressing the knife harder, his warm breath and lips brushed her earlobe. "I'm going to move my hand, Dreamer. Try to scream, and I'll slit your throat." He jerked her hair, forcing her to look at his face. An evil grin spread his lips.

Cyrus.

"What the hell. Go ahead and scream. No one would hear you, and your screams would please me."

No wonder she found him so attractive. Bad habit of hers. Always drawn to assholes. Damn shame, she was going to have to kick his ass.

The Legacy taught her well. Like all Dreamers, she was trained in all forms of fighting from the time she could walk. Although the healing powers of her Dreamer body would have been a bonus, she was sure she could give this prick a run for his money. Collecting her thoughts, she focused, preparing her body for the oncoming battle. All senses on high alert.

He shoved her forward.

Landing on her hands, she kicked her legs up and out, her heavy boots thumping against his head. Not giving him a chance to react, she crouched low and rolled between his legs, slamming her fist upward into his balls with all her might.

Her courage faltered when, instead of screaming in pain, he reached down and grabbed her by the neck, lifting her until she was eye level.

"Finished yet, little girl?" He sneered, squeezing off her airway.

I will not pass out. She repeated the mantra in her head until it wasn't his hand on her neck controlling her breath. It was her will. Clawing at his fingers with one hand, she reached under her shirt with the other, clutching the brass handled dagger concealed in the sheath attached to her waistband. She rammed the blade into his neck, blood splattering her face and body.

Cyrus threw her over the couch, her body crashing into the coffee table, her dagger skittered across the floor.

She landed in a heap, but immediately got on all fours. Trying not to focus on her battered neck, she gulped in as much air as she could. Snatching up the letter opener that fell to the floor, she returned to her feet.

Leaping over the broken table, she hurled all her weight at her bleeding enemy while he was still off balance. She sank the tip of the dragon handled opener into his cheek and jerked down, laying open the skin.

He batted her away from him as if she was nothing more than an annoying chihuahua yapping at a pit-bull.

Landing on her back, she gaped in horror as his cheek and temple immediately healed. "You can't be." She crab walked backward, clawing the carpet, searching for anything to use as a weapon. "How can you be a Dreamer? You're a man. You wear the ring of a Catcher."

He smirked. "This ring belongs to the Catcher I killed."

"No." She shook her head. "How can you? The ring's not glowing."

"You're a traitor, Dreamer." He stalked her with an evil grin. "Yes, that will be your new name. Traitor. You betrayed the Legacy, and your sister Dreamers. Because of you and your kind, Dreamers died."

He kneeled down to whisper in her ear. "Do you remember Dannen?"

Astrid froze, the memory of her late friend's face contorted in agony clear in her mind. It had been over four years since Astrid found her friend dead in her bed. An autopsy showed Dannen died of a heart attack. Of course, there was an investigation. It's not every day a healthy twenty-seven-year-old woman dies of a heart failure.

Astrid knew a Catcher was involved. Dannen had an assignment the previous night. She wasn't supposed to engage the mark. Apparently, the Catcher got the drop on her.

Die in your dreams, die in real life.

She'd begged Dannen to leave the Dreamer life with her. She was tired of killing, blindly following orders of the Legacy. But Dannen wouldn't listen. The Dreamer lifestyle was the only one she knew, and she didn't want to leave. They'd had a fierce argument about it. It's why Astrid had gone to see her.

"You...you killed her," Astrid stammered. "Why?"

"No," Cyrus growled. "She died because of you. You should have been there with her. The Catcher who killed her could never have taken her down had the two of you been together.

"If you're a Dreamer, you know that's not possible. We can't work in pairs." Astrid glared at him, feeling around for the dagger. "Besides, as a man, you *have* to be a Catcher. Dannen was a Dreamer. Why do you care that a Dreamer was killed?"

Her hand touched the dagger on the floor behind her. She rose to her knees, the brass and steel balanced perfectly for her hand, and hurled it at Cyrus's chest.

Cyrus caught the knife, then disappeared.

What the hell? Where did he go?

He reappeared next to her, punched her in the face, then rammed the knife into her side.

The world blended into a myriad of colors and shapes. Blood poured from her nose, and she sank to the floor. Against all logic, she crawled along the floor on her belly.

There was no escaping him.

She turned over on her back and struck out wildly, her heart beating in an unfamiliar rhythm. An old feeling covered her in an uncomfortable shroud. One she hadn't experienced since she was a child. An emotion that had been stripped from her as part of her training.

Intense Fear.

"We're going on a journey, traitor. There's a little game we're going to play. Winner takes all." Cyrus straddled her legs, but she couldn't feel his weight. "We're going to see Lucien Drake. He needs to tell Stephen Prescott that Cyrus is in town. Somiar and Lucien need to get their affairs in order. They don't know it yet, but they're already dead," he snickered. "Daddy's home, but he won't be able to save them."

Astrid fought to stay conscious. "Why? Why are you doing this? You have no reason to side with Dreamers. What's in it for you?"

Cyrus bent over her, his face so close she could feel his breath. "I'm a Dreamer, bitch."

"You can't be. You're a man. Dreamers can't change gender." *What the hell is going on?* She barely registered the sharp prick at her lower neck. So, he did know the weakness of the Dreamers. Now that he'd pinned her, she wouldn't be able to move, or summon her Dreamer body. She could see his fist coming toward her face but could do nothing to stop him. Pain ripped through her head.

Unable to stay awake. She drowned in the abyss.

***

Astrid wasn't sure how much time had gone by. There was an odd sensation of movement, like being on an airplane when it first takes off. She blinked several times, trying to clear her vision, but could only see blurred shapes. Her body tossed against plush leather, sore, and wanting the jostling to stop.

As if someone heard her wish, there was slowing, then stillness.

"We're here, traitor." Cyrus spoke in a conversational tone. Almost friendly. "You'd better hope Lucien's home. You don't look so good."

She heard the opening and closing of a car door. A breeze ruffled her hair when the door on her side opened.

Her body screamed in agony when Cyrus seized her under both arms and dragged her out of the car onto the pavement, but she refused to let any sound escape her lips.

"Don't forget my message, bitch. They're all dead."

Without another word, he was back in his car.

She wasn't sure if it was real, or her battered mind, but the car seemed to disappear in mid-air.

"Stay conscious," she mumbled as she staggered up the stone driveway. Making it to the massive iron gates, she pressed the intercom button, leaving a bloody print on the numbered panel.

Please, God, let him be home.

The pain in her side made it hard to breathe. She pressed her hand to the wound, hoping to slow the red river flowing down her waist onto her jeans. The metallic odor of blood filled her nostrils. She fought the bile bubbling in her throat, threatening to add to the sticky mess on her clothes.

The slight hum from the intercom caught her attention. Seconds later, a small yellow light blinked on a camera above the gate.

"Who are you and what do you want?" asked the deep, irritated male voice.

"Lucien Drake?" Astrid licked her dry lips. Dehydration was setting in and the ground tilted under her. She leaned against the gate and held onto the control panel. "My name is Astrid Beal. Help me."

"I'm calling the police and an ambulance. Just stay where you are." His words came out in a panicked rush.

Astrid fought down her fear. The last thing she needed was her heart rate to go up, making her blood loss more intense. "No, please. No police. I'm a Dreamer. Help me." Her legs buckled and peaceful blackness followed.

***

Lucien sprinted out of his bedroom, tugging his bathrobe over his nude body as he went.

What the hell was a battered, bloody Dreamer doing outside his gate in the middle of the night? And why hadn't she healed herself?

He yanked the keys to his Aston Martin off the hook in the kitchen and tore open the door leading to the garage, not bothering to close it behind him.

If she was as bad as she looked, there was no way could he carry her dead weight up the half mile drive to the house. The garage door was barely open when he stomped on the accelerator and sped down the driveway.

He tapped the voice command on the dash. A polite female voice asked what he would like to do.

"Call Malachi."

In seconds, Malachi's deep voice let loose on him. "Lucien, I swear if this isn't life or death, I'm going to kick..."

"You and Somiar need to get your asses over here *now*. I've got a half dead woman in front of my house claiming to be a Dreamer." He didn't give Malachi a chance to respond before he disconnected the call.

Pulling up to the closed gate, he could barely make out the motionless form on the other side. He cut his headlights, not wanting to attract attention to any cars that may pass by. His house was on the dead-end street, and at this late hour the chances of someone coming down the road was slim, but he didn't want to press his luck.

After pounding in the access code, he jumped out of the car and through the narrow passage of the slowly opening gate.

He kneeled next to the crumpled heap and put two fingers to her neck. Her pulse was slow and thready, her breathing shallow. There was blood everywhere, so he had no idea where she was injured. He ran his hand over her body, inhaling deeply when he felt the deep hole in her side.

Placing his hands over the wound, he closed his eyes and imagined the hole getting smaller. The burning in his hands let him know his powers were working. The blood on the sidewalk and her clothes faded.

He healed her just enough to keep her alive, but not to enough to wake her from her unconscious state. Running back to the car, he grabbed a Dreamer pin. He leaned down to insert it into the side of her neck. He finished healing her then placed her in the passenger side, using the seat belt to hold her upright.

Once they reached the house, he carried her to the living room.

"Thank God, you're alright. I popped in as soon as you called."

Lucien almost dropped the woman in his arms at the sound of his sister's voice behind him.

"Dammit, Somiar, how many times have I told you not to do that! You scared the shit out of me." Lucien placed the woman on the couch and turned to face her.

Somiar crossed her arms in front of her chest. "You're the one who called *my* house in the middle of the night. Leila took the kids tonight so Malachi and I could have some alone time. First time since the triplets were born. Malachi is on his way." She stood next to the couch and smirked at the slumbering figure resting there. "Thanks a lot, whoever you are," she scoffed.

"She said her name is Astrid Beal. She knew my name, but I've never seen her before."

"There's something familiar about her." Somiar frowned. "Are you sure she's a Dreamer? Why didn't she heal herself?"

"Because this isn't her Dreamer body. Whoever did this to her had to have done it while she was awake." Lucien rubbed his chin. "But she *is* a Dreamer. I was able to heal her."

Somiar cocked her head and pressed a finger to her lip. "You pinned her?"

"Yeah." Lucien kneeled next to the couch and positioned Astrid's head to the side, exposing her neck and the star-shaped pin attached to the skin. He took a moment to inspect his guest.

Her coal black hair was a tangled mess, and her ebony skin was streaked with dirt. Although the blood that had been covering her clothes had disappeared, they were still a muddy, grimy disaster.

The screech of tires, followed by a car door slamming, saved him from having to comment further.

A few seconds later, Malachi rushed into the room. "Lucien, are you alright?"

At Lucien's nod, he stepped to his wife's side and peered at the woman lying peacefully on the couch. "This her?" Malachi stroked his chin. "She must have a pretty good story about why she came here, of all places. What Dreamer seeks a Catcher when she's in trouble?"

"It could be a trap." Somiar put her arm around her husband's waist. "The Legacy has been way too quiet lately, but I can't figure why they'd send her here. They know this place is a fortress against Dreamers. Not even mom can get in without one of us."

"Only one way to find out." Lucien bent and withdrew the Dreamer pin from Astrid's neck and stood back.

Her eyes popped open, and she jerked up.

"Hey there, sleeping beauty." Lucien took care to keep his voice steady. "Want to tell us what's going on?"

***

Blinking several times to bring the room into focus, Astrid tried to make sense of her surroundings. Running a hand over her body, she realized her wounds were gone, and she was pain free. Aside from the thick fog clouding her brain, she felt fine.

She surveyed the trio staring curiously at her. She didn't expect to wake up to this.

Her gaze settled on the man seated on the coffee table in front of her. Never had she seen a man so drop dead gorgeous. Chocolate silk skin, light brown eyes. His full, luscious lips were what wet dreams were made of. A neatly trimmed goatee and mustache gave him a mature, sexy vibe.

Something about the way he looked at her made her uneasy. With a quick glance at his hands, she noticed the absence of a Catcher's ring. If he weren't a Catcher, he should have called the cops the moment she showed up in his driveway.

The only thing she could do was deliver the message and hope she didn't have to fight her way out of this nightmare. "I need to speak to Stephen. Stephen Prescott."

"Why?" The deep timbre of his voice came at a low rumble. It was pleasant, almost soothing. His gaze held hers, his brown eyes giving nothing away.

"His life is in danger." Astrid leaned back against the couch. "I was attacked in my house by a man named Cyrus. He told me to make sure I don't die before Stephen got his message. Something about Somiar and Lucien are already dead."

She studied his face, looking for some indication that he knew what she was talking about. His expression remained impassive.

"You were out cold when I found you at my gate. How'd you get here?"

"Cyrus. He's responsible for all of this. When I woke up, he was leaving me on the sidewalk. I didn't think I could make it." She leaned in closer to get a better look at her host. "Oh, my God. You're *that* Lucien. You healed me, didn't you?"

Lucien shot her a narrowed glance. "What do you mean *that* Lucien? What's going on?"

Astrid wasn't sure how much she should tell him. After all, he wasn't the one trying to kill her. But she couldn't be sure. The Legacy let her leave the life way too easily, so she had to always watch her back. As far as she knew, this could be their way of using her to get to him.

"Every Dreamer knows about you. News of your existence, and your sister's..." her gaze went to Somiar, "unique circumstances, traveled fast. Children of a Dreamer and Catcher. You both are considered abominations in the eyes of the Legacy."

Lucien's lips pressed flat. "So why should I trust anything you say? I don't know anyone named Cyrus, and I don't know you."

The other man in the room stepped forward. "No need to be rude, Lucien." He turned to Astrid, his smile not reaching his eyes. "May I present my wife, Somiar. I'm Malachi. You seem to have the answers to all our questions."

His conversational tone didn't fool Astrid for one minute.

She knew exactly who he was, and his nice guy attitude was an insult. Malachi Walker was known to all Dreamers as one of the most ruthless Catchers, second only to Lucien and Somiar's father, Richard Drake. Richard's death elevated Malachi to public enemy number one with Dreamers. Strange, such a staunch enemy married a Dreamer.

"I knew who all of you were before the introductions. Like I said, the story of you, and the Legacy traveled fast. Who the bad guys were depended on who told the story. But I'm afraid I don't know what's going on, who Cyrus is, or why I was the one chosen to deliver this message. I haven't been part of the Dreamer's way of life in years."

Lucien turned to Somiar. "Get Stephen on the com. He and Leila need to be in the loop."

Astrid studied the group, all taking their cues from Lucien. She had no idea who Stephen was, and looked forward to finally having a piece of her cryptic message solved.

Somiar went to the computer panel and tapped the necessary keys. A few seconds later, a rather handsome gentleman with curly salt and pepper hair appeared on a large screen mounted on the wall.

The woman next to him, though obviously older, bore a startling resemblance to Somiar. No doubt, she was their mother.

"It's been confirmed. The woman Lucien found is a Dreamer," said Somiar.

The man she assumed was Stephen ran his fingers through his hair. "What the hell is a Dreamer doing in his house? You should have put her on ice and sent her to a Catcher station. I swear, you young people are going to turn my hair completely gray."

"If you'd calm down a moment, maybe we can get a handle on what's going on." Malachi made a quick introduction and briefed him on the situation.

Stephen stroked the hairs on his chin. "I'm lost. I don't know anyone named Cyrus." He glanced at the woman at his side. "What about you, Lee?"

"Never heard of him." Her husky voice was barely above a whisper.

Something about Lee's countenance made Astrid uneasy. It was almost like she was looking through her. Like they had something in common, but she wasn't willing to share what it was.

Stephen turned his attention back to Astrid. "Why don't you start from the beginning."

Astrid sat with her legs folded under her and rubbed her temples. "Tonight wasn't the first time I'd seen him. He was at 'Roll With It' last night, too. We get a lot of regulars, so I didn't think anything of it."

"Roll with it?" Malichi knitted his brow.

"Sushi restaurant in Buckhead," Lucien supplied. "They have out of this world sushi and sashimi." He studied Astrid for a moment, then snapped his fingers. "I knew I'd seen you before. In Black Diamonds magazine. You own 'Roll With It' and 'The Silver Lotus'."

He turned back to Malachi. "Remember a while back, I suggested we try to get a 'Silver Lotus' franchise at Luna?"

Malachi nodded and Lucien pointed to Astrid. "This woman employs the most talented Asian chefs in Atlanta."

"I still don't understand why she was the chosen messenger. The Legacy has been silent for three years. Why resurface now?" Malachi shot Astrid a wary glance. "And why you?"

Astrid held up a hand. "Wait a minute. I didn't say the Legacy had anything to do with this. The person who attacked me is a man. He claimed to be a Dreamer, but Dreamers can't change gender, and I'm sure they'd never use a man as an ally."

She didn't miss the quick exchange of looks from the others in the room. Her eyes narrowed. "What am I missing? What aren't you telling me?"

Lucien leaned in closer to Astrid. "It's too early in the game for you to be asking us questions. What's the message Cyrus wanted you to deliver?"

She ran her tongue across her dry lips. "Daddy's home, but he can't save you."

"What kind of weird shit is that?" Lucien turned to Somiar, and raised a brow. "Any idea what that means?"

Somiar frowned, and scoffed, "Your guess is as good as mine."

"Maybe we should get her to the Catcher station. We could get a description and run the name in the Catcher database. Cyrus isn't an overly common name." Lucien picked up his phone.

"Oh, no you don't." Astrid attempted to stand but was stopped by Lucien's hand on her shoulder.

"You need to stay seated." Lucien's tone left no room for discussion. "There's no way in hell we're giving you free rein right now."

Astrid's jaw tightened "I know what Catchers do to Dreamers. I'll go to sleep and won't wake up for weeks." How the hell was she going to get out of this? She didn't trust them anymore than they trusted her, but they held all the cards right now.

"If you know our story, then you know we've been trying to bring Dreamers and Catchers together for the last few years," Malachi said. "It hasn't been easy. We're still not willing to trust each other, and to be honest, it isn't practical right now. Too much bad blood and history of us trying to kill each other."

"Exactly. I know your story. And I know the Legacy's story. What makes you so much more trustworthy?" Astrid nibbled on the inside of her lip.

Truth be told, a lot of Dreamers felt the same way. But it was Catchers who hunted them like vermin. They claimed their hunting of Dreamers as a necessary evil.

It was the Legacy who made sure Dreamers could thrive, despite interference from Catchers. Although being an assassin left a rancid taste in her mouth, she did what she had to do in order to survive. And sometimes that meant taking the lives of some hugely unsavory people.

"Because you don't have a choice. Do you really want to go out there and take your chances with the psycho who dumped you in my driveway?" Lucien's sardonic smile impaled her. "Besides, your story could be bullshit. The Legacy has a reputation for being extremely resourceful. How do we know you're not a plant?"

Astrid gave him a level stare. "Are you saying I'm a prisoner? Don't you think people will try to find me? You don't think my employees, at both restaurants, aren't going to notice I'm missing?"

"We're not going to hold you prisoner." Lucien manifested a casual tone and a disingenuous smile. "We want to invite you to the Catchers station for a couple of days. See if we can get some answers. If we wanted to hurt you, do you think we'd be having this discussion?"

Astrid couldn't argue with that. Time to choose between the lesser of two evils. "I'll go with you, but I need to talk to my assistant. She knows I wouldn't disappear without giving her a heads up. I'll tell her I'm taking a vacation or something. If I could borrow your phone?"

"I've got a better idea." Lucien went into another room and returned with a flip phone. "Use this one. Untraceable."

Astrid smirked. "A burner phone?"

"Why would I give you mine? I don't know you, or your assistant."

Astrid took the phone and tapped the necessary numbers. It went straight to voicemail. "Listen, Casey, I'm going to take a few days off. Stay away from sexy pants. I get the feeling he's a total asshole."

She rolled her eyes at Lucien's raised brow. "My therapist says I'm burning myself out and need to relax a bit, so I'm at a retreat to unplug. No phones, or internet unless it's an extreme emergency. I'll be back Monday morning, so I need you to take care of things until then." She disconnected and gave the phone back to Lucien.

Lucien shot her a sidelong glance. "Sexy pants?"

Astrid folded her arms in front of her chest. "Cyrus. She saw him in the restaurant. Not a good idea to tell her he tried to kill me. She knows nothing of Dreamers and Catchers and I plan to keep it that way."

A hint of a smile softened his face. "Your therapist said you need to take time off? That's the story you used?'"

"I couldn't use the family emergency excuse, I have no family. But I do have a therapist. Besides, she'll be wondering why I didn't call from my phone." Astrid quirked a brow. "You have seven days to find what you need before she gets suspicious."

Malachi took a step forward and addressed Stephen. "Since this case fell in Lucien's lap, he should take lead. It's time."

Stephen nodded. "He can take lead, but I want you guiding him."

"Got it." Malachi gave Lucien a rueful smile. "Congrats. You got your first full-fledged assignment. Welcome to hell."

Chapter 2

A strid lifted her head from the wooden table, eyelids heavy, her mouth tasting like she'd sucked on a cotton lollipop. Being pinned was part of training during her years as a young Dreamer, but this was the first time she'd been pinned multiple times in a twenty-four-hour period.

Lucien sat across from her, his face impassive, waiting for her to focus.

Astrid suppressed the emotions wanting to surface. Dreamers law, never show emotion. Every training session started and ended with that lesson. She fingered the sore spot on her neck. "How many times are you going to stick that damned thing in my neck? It's starting to piss me off."

Lucien moved to her side and placed his hand over the puncture wounds at her neck. "Now that you're here at the center, we won't have to. Unless you give us reason to put you on ice and keep you there."

She winced at the burning sensation as he healed her and tried not to react when he softly blew on the spot, attempting to cool her skin.

She felt a tinge of disappointment when he returned to the other side of the table.

"And what do you consider a reason?" Astrid surveyed the room. It was large, the walls a pretty peacock blue, an oversized king bed against the far wall dominated the room. A bright chandelier hung over the bed, calla lilies and freesias tucked in small corners, but not so much that the scent was overwhelming. "What's with the bed? Taking an awful lot for granted, aren't you?"

"I don't plan on taking anything." Lucien's face remained aloof, though there was a hint of amusement in his voice. "This will be your room while you're our guest. The only thing I want from you is information."

He ran his finger across the smooth mahogany desk separating them. "Someone connected to you has threatened my family." His lips spread in a thin line. The only menacing expression from him she'd seen all evening. "And that shit ain't cool."

"What *ain't cool*, is that he broke into my house, beat the crap out of me, and dumped me in your driveway." She stood and paced the floor, very aware his gaze never left her. "Besides the fact that he's... well... a *he?* The man disappeared and reappeared in a different place in the room."

Lucien cocked his head and raised a brow. "So, now you're going to make up stories. You had me up to the disappearing act."

Astrid narrowed her eyes and retook her seat across from him. "Yeah. I had *him* up to the disappearing act too. The fact that a man claimed to be a Dreamer doesn't surprise you?"

She searched his face for some sign, anything that would give her some insight as to what the hell was going on. "Come on, dude. Spill it. You know as well as I that all Dreamers are women. What's going on?"

A sly smile crept across his face that set her skin crawling. "You're in no position to ask questions." He headed for the white door next to the bed. "The closet is fully stocked with casual and workout clothes. I assume the women got your size correct. You have half an hour to shower and change."

"Half hour until wha----"

Lucien left the room and closed the door before she could finish her sentence.

***

"I believe her." Lucien sat back in his chair and looked at his sister and brother-in-law on one of several wall mounted screens across the room. "We never disclosed that a Dreamer, a *male* Dreamer attacked Stephen four years ago. And the Legacy has been way too quiet."

"She could be working with him," Somiar interjected. "What bothers me is something about this seems personal, and I think Stephen is the key. The message about us, was for him to hear."

The light and airy musical tone from the speaker next to the door interrupted them. Lucien glanced at the camera on his desk to see an irritated looking Astrid and her guards. "I guess we're about to get some answers. I'll keep the two of you posted."

At Malachi's nod, Lucien tapped the button on a remote. A panel slid in place, concealing the monitor. With the punch of another button, the door glided open.

Although Astrid was escorted by a Catcher behind her and another in front, she still managed to stroll in like she owned the place. "I feel like I'm on an episode of Star Trek."

Lucien worked to keep his expression blank. "We told you where you are. If we're to get through this, you have to be up front with us."

He had to hand it to Astrid. She didn't bat an eye at his matter-of-fact tone. He slid a large black binder to the center of the table. "We want you to go through this book. It's a list of Dreamers."

"Dreamers?" Astrid rolled her eyes and sighed. "I told you. This person is a man, and you know there are no male Dreamers."

"Are you sure he was a man?"

She folded her arms and shot Lucien a stare that could freeze a desert. "Well, the person I fought last night sure as hell wasn't a woman. When I jackhammered his nuts, I definitely felt balls. Even if he were a woman, being hit that hard in the pussy would have made one hell of an impact."

Lucien fought the urge to cover his crotch with his hands at the thought of his balls being pummeled. He opened the cover to the first page. "Humor me."

***

Astrid flipped through the pages, trying not to wince when she came across a few of her fellow Dreamers. Each one had labels attached.

Sola: on ice.

Lana: on ice.

Canary: killed trying to escape.

Some were labeled as still at large with no picture, only the crime they'd committed. Like her, they'd never been captured, photographed, or named. The instinct to beat the shit out of her captors bubbled in her chest. Some of the Dreamers listed had been missing for years. She couldn't imagine being kept in a state of oblivion for that long. Were they ever revived? How were they kept healthy?

"Are the Dreamers on ice kept here?" She tried to keep her tone casual.

"That's none of your concern." A muscle jerked in Lucien's jaw. "Keep looking."

Slamming the book shut, Astrid rubbed at her tired eyes. "This isn't going to work. I'm looking for a man, and you've given me a book full of women."

"Then we have to find another way." Lucien stroked his chin. "There's no way in hell I'm letting you see who our Catchers are."

Astrid was about to hurl a scathing retort when the door slid open.

Somiar rushed into the room, waving a large piece of paper, Malachi not far behind, waited just inside the door. She headed straight for Astrid, and slammed the page on the table in front of her. "Is this the description you gave our artists?"

Astrid peered at the image. "Wow. When your artist did the drawing, it wasn't this good. But, yeah, this is the guy."

"A preliminary sketch could look like several people. Our computer attempts to fill in the blanks when given a rough description. We ran it through our image program, and got a hit." Somiar pressed a button imbedded in the wall at the end of the room. A panel in the wall slid back to reveal a monitor. After tapping a few keys on what looked like a remote, the screen lit up.

The image of a funeral played out across the screen. The man Astrid recognized as Stephen from their meeting last night, was on his cell, when another man ran past and hurled a knife at him. It zipped through his flesh leaving a deep gash in his cheek.

Somiar froze the image and zoomed in on the man who'd thrown the knife.

"What the fuck is going on!" Lucien swore. "That's the guy who attacked Stephen at Monica's funeral."

Astrid's eyes widened. "The same Stephen I met last night?" She continued to watch the screen, fascinated by the scene playing out in front of her. "Seems to me, he tried to deliver the message himself and ya'll didn't take the hint."

"Apparently." Somiar dropped the remote on the table. "Listen little brother, I know you wanted to keep the drama at a minimum, but Leila and Stephen need to know what's going on."

Lucien scoffed. "You know they're going to lose their shit when we let them in on this."

Somiar retreated behind the door, then reappeared seconds later. "Malachi's delivering the message and is on the way here."

"What are you talking about? Malachi's already here," Astrid said. She turned and surveyed the room. "Wait, I know I saw him here just a minute ago." She narrowed her eyes and turned back to Somiar. "You're using your Dreamer body."

Somiar slid her a sly smile.

"But, Malachi's not a Dreamer. How did he…" Astrid's brows knit. "Hold on. I remember being briefed on this. You can pull him to you. Where you go, you can bring him with you." She snapped her fingers. "Maybe that's how Cyrus did it. That's how he healed himself. He has a Dreamer helping him."

"No." Somiar shook her head. "Dreamers can't heal other people. They can only heal themselves." She gave a wry chuckle. "If you really want to scramble your brain, only Catchers who have a Dreamer mother and Catcher father can heal other Catchers and Dreamers.

"As far as we know, the war between the Dreamers and Catchers caused such a hatred for each other, they never mated. Lucien and my sons are the only ones who fit that category. Besides, Catchers can't heal themselves. You said Cyrus healed himself."

Astrid sat back with a loud sigh. "Healing himself is a Dreamer power, but men can't be Dreamers." She rubbed her temples, the whole mess giving her a massive headache. "And that thing he did with disappearing and reappearing in plain view still has me stumped. Not even Dreamers can do that."

She leaned back, gazing at the ceiling as if the answer would suddenly appear. Racking her brain for a detail. Some small, missing piece that would turn this enigma into a clear picture.

"I'm lost. So far, the only thing we know about this guy is he attacked Stephen and I, years apart. It doesn't make sense. This guy attacked a Dreamer and a Catcher. What's the connection?"

Astrid thought back to their fight in her house. "He kept calling me a traitor to Dreamers and the Legacy." She gazed at Somiar. "I remember seeing footage of your mother's funeral."

"She wasn't my mother," Somiar interjected through clenched teeth. "That monster wasn't my mother. Leila is my mother."

"I know she put you through hell, and I have no idea what that was like. But the world, including me, knew Monica as your mother." Astrid sighed. "The knife incident was never aired. No one even remembers it happening. The Legacy figured the Catchers had the spectator's minds wiped. The world didn't know about Monica being a Legacy member, but I'm sure her funeral was crawling with Catchers, just in case any of the Legacy showed up."

"Does this replay have a point?" It was Lucien's turn to interrupt.

"Why would Cyrus do this? It's obvious he didn't want Stephen dead. And why did he attack Stephen and not you? Or Somiar? You two are the real threat to the Legacy." Astrid leveled a gaze at Somiar. "And now, so are your children."

Somiar advanced on Astrid. "Are you threatening my children?"

Astrid rose to her feet and held her ground, knowing if this came to blows, there was no way would she win. She would be fighting a Dreamer using her Dreamer body, in a setting full of people who would protect Somiar at all cost. She held Somiar's gaze and clenched her teeth. "No. But you need to find out who is. And I don't think it's the Legacy."

"Now you've got me confused." Lucien's voice cut the crackling tension between the two women. "Why wouldn't it be the Legacy?"

"Because as soon as that man showed his face, they would have cut out his tongue and turned him to a eunuch before they killed him." Her gaze slid from Somiar to Lucien.

"I find it hard to believe they'd have such disdain for someone doing their dirty work for them. Sounds to me like he'd be more of an asset." Lucien traced an invisible pattern on his desk, "He'd be the perfect fall guy."

"Have you bumped your head? This guy is impersonating one of them. That's not something they'd take lightly. Do you really think they'd hire a man to do anything for them?" Astrid glanced at Somiar. "Come on, I know you weren't brought up with us, but damn, you must know *something* about the life."

"Us?" Lucien stabbed her with a sharp glare. "I though you said you left the life."

"I did." Astrid glared back. What was it with this family and staring contests? "But I am what I am. I was born a Dreamer, and that's what I'll always be. I chose not to continue working in the life, but that doesn't mean I've forgotten everything I was taught."

Lucien folded his arms across his chest. "Yeah, I'll bet you have." His voice dripped with sarcasm.

Ignoring his remark, Astrid continued. "The Legacy, and Dreamers, view men as a necessary, but pleasurable evil to procreate. The moment a man becomes a liability, they're collateral damage. Tossed out like junk mail. They're usually set up as the victim of a drug deal gone wrong. That way, there's no public sympathy for him. Just another drug dealer, or addict, who got what he deserved."

Lucien sucked a breath through his teeth and shot her a caustic glare. "Seems like it's not just Somiar and I who are considered abominations."

Astrid did a mental count to ten. "Will you let me finish, or are you going to continue to sulk because the Legacy said something mean about you?"

At his curt nod, she continued. "I suspect you know as much about the Legacy as the rest of the Catchers. Men aren't meant to be anything more than a good time or a sperm donor. That's why most Dreamers don't know who their fathers are."

"Trust me when I tell you, that's not a smart move. Had I known who my father was, we wouldn't be in this mess." Somiar moved to stand at Lucien's side. "My brother and I could have grown up together. No animosity, and our father might still be alive."

"So, we're back at square one. No way is this man a Dreamer, and he definitely wasn't hired by the Legacy. Are you all sure he's not a Catcher?" Astrid asked.

"Absolutely." Lucien spoke up. "We checked him out when he pulled that shit at the funeral. He's definitely not a Catcher."

Astrid resumed her seat and massaged her temples, thinking back to the fight in her house. "Dannen. He blamed me for Dannen's death."

Lucien's head snapped up. "Your old roommate? She's been dead for years. What's she got to do with any of this?"

Astrid opened her mouth then snapped her lips shut. Of course, they would know about Dannen. They probably knew everything about her by now. "I don't see how she would have anything to do with this."

Lucien absently stroked his chin with his index finger. "We know she's a Dreamer and died on assignment. Killed by a Catcher. We never did figure out who her mark was."

Astrid scoffed. "Is she in your little book of horrors too?"

"Yes." Lucien's tone held no remorse. He opened the book and flipped it to Dannen's page. "I see nothing in here that would tie her to anyone named Cyrus."

Astrid stared down at her friend's photos. School pictures, high school, and college graduation. She and Astrid getting henna tattoos on their feet at the dogwood festival in Piedmont Park. Laying on her bed, lifeless eyes open, staring sightlessly.

Astrid gasped and slammed the book closed, then turned away from the siblings, wrapping her arms around her mid-section. It took everything in her not to lash out and scream at them.

"Listen, I'm sorry. That wasn't necessary." Lucien came up and put a hand on her shoulder.

Not giving her own safety a second thought, she whirled around, grabbed his arm, and kicked his legs out from under him. Surprised when no one stopped her, she came down on her knees next to him. "Touch me again, and I swear I'll kill you." She stood and faced Somiar. "I want to leave. Now. I have nothing else to say."

The door opened and the same man who brought her to the room stepped in. He raised a brow when he spotted Lucien on the floor. Barely stifling a chuckle, he glanced at Astrid. "Come with me."

Before the door closed behind her, she heard Somiar's voice. "That was a shitty thing to do. You deserved to be dropped on your ass."

CHAPTER 3

Astrid stared at the ceiling in the room she'd been assigned. She wasn't sure how long they would keep her here, but at least they'd made sure she was comfortable. Hell, had it not been for the knowledge that two big, burly Catchers guarded her door, she may have been able to relax.

Her room was lined with bookshelves, crammed with books from all genres. "Well, at least I won't get bored," she murmured, fingering the leather binders.

She pulled one from the shelf and returned to her bed. *Killing Delilah.* She read the short blurb on the back of the book and turned to the first page. After reading the same three pages several times without retaining a word, she placed the book on the bedside table and closed her eyes to meditate.

Breath one. Toes, feet, calves, and thighs relax. Breath two. Torso shoulders, arms relax. Breath three. Neck mouth eyes... Her body began to float. Once her feet touched the floor, she opened her eyes.

She glanced over at her sleeping body and leaned against her door. Aware that her captors were probably watching her every move, she wondered why they allowed her to keep her Dreamer ability instead of putting her on ice.

Cautiously opening the door, she glanced at each of her guards, lounging against the wall across from her room. She summed them up, wondering if she could take them, now that she had the added bonus of her Dreamer body. She'd learned to heal herself quickly, so maybe she stood a chance against them.

Curious as to why they made no move to stop her from leaving the room, she put one foot beyond the threshold.

Pain raced from her foot throughout the rest of her body the moment she stepped across the seam where her gray carpet ended and the gleaming white tile in the hallway began. She crumpled to the floor gasping from the pain. Question answered. They knew she wouldn't be able to leave the room in her Dreamer form.

"Oops. Our bad. We forgot to lock your door." The muscle-bound, bald man had a deep, rumbling voice. "We suggest you stay in your room. And be careful. Getting zapped too many times can be bad for your heart."

The other guard, a tall, dark man, gave her a passing glance before resuming his nonchalant pose against the wall. The deadly gleam in his eyes told her he wasn't as relaxed as he seemed.

She closed the door and half crawled to the oversized leather chair in the corner. She climbed to the center and curled up, regaining her breath. "You can stop playing your sick little games now. I get it. I'm not going anywhere." Straightening up, she raised her voice. "I know you're listening. I wouldn't mind a little company."

She leaned her head against the armrest, the gravity of her situation dawning on her.

A knock on her door made her jump. She stood in the middle of the floor, trying to look like the picture of composure.

Lucien strode into the room, pushing a trolley cart bearing a pot of tea, and a variety of packed sub sandwiches.

His tall stance and muscular body would definitely make a woman look twice. His black t-shirt hugged his broad chest. Denim clad thighs gave her thoughts that made her forget her situation.

"When I can't sleep, I raid the fridge," he said without preamble. He glanced at her sleeping body, then back at her. "I forgot that lack of sleep isn't a problem for Dreamers."

Astrid shrugged. "It's not for a lot of us. I figured it would be best to let my body rest so I don't crash and burn in the next few days."

"Well, according to my sister, your mind has to rest too." He poured a cup of tea and handed it to Astrid. "Orange lavender. It's supposed to help with relaxation, but I guess it doesn't matter, seeing that it won't affect you in this state."

"No, it won't, but I still love the taste." She sipped the tea and grabbed a sandwich. "Club subs. Glad you're not the vegan sandwich type." She took a large, unladylike bite and sat back in her chair,

Feet tucked under her, she motioned at his hand. "I notice you never wear a Catcher's ring. How come?"

Lucien sat in the chair next to hers. He tore open a packet of mustard, concentrating way too hard on adding the condiment and refused to meet her gaze. "I don't need my ring to tell me you're a Dreamer. We already know that. Besides, your Dreamer body would have that thing glowing like crazy right now. It'd be kind of annoying, don't you think?"

"I guess so. I assumed you guys never took them off." She cocked her head to the side, trying to figure out why he seemed so uncomfortable about his ring. "So, why are you awake?"

He set his cup on the table between them. "I wanted to apologize for what I did earlier today." He ran his hand across the back of his neck, shoulders slouched. "My sister really let me have it once you left. It wasn't so long ago I was given no regard, treated like I didn't matter. I'm sorry I did that to you."

Astrid wasn't sure she was ready to let him off the hook so easily, so she changed the subject. "Can I ask you a question?"

He raised his head and turned to her. "Sure."

"Why aren't I on ice? I know the place is secure, but I could still be a threat."

"We only put Dreamers on ice who've done something to warrant it. As far as we know, you're just as much a target as the rest of us." He rubbed his chin. "What we don't know is why."

"But how do you know I'm not trying to trick you? I could be trying to get an inside track to take you down."

He chuckled. "If that's the case, you're pretty bad at it to sit there and bring up the possibility. Or maybe that makes you a genius. Either way, we're not fools. We got you covered. Don't ask how, because that's our business."

"Got it." Stretching her legs out in front of her, and taking another sip of her tea, she studied his features. If only they weren't in this situation. She'd love to see what was under those clothes. Remembering her track record, she decided he must be a scumbag.

"Is something wrong?" he asked.

"No." She brushed an imaginary speck off her sweatpants when she realized she'd been caught staring. "I've been thinking. There's got to be a connection between Dannen, Stephen, and your family. Cyrus mentioned all of you."

"I guess it's as good a place as any to start."

She nibbled on her lower lip. "Can I ask for a favor?"

"You may as well. All I can do is say yes or no."

"I know you must have a training facility somewhere in this building. Can I have a couple of hours a day in it? If there's a lunatic out there after me, the last thing I need is to allow myself to get out of shape."

Lucien nodded. "That's not a problem. Besides, Somiar could use a little practice sparring with someone other than mom and the Catchers."

"Will we be able to use our Dreamer bodies?"

Lucien thought for a minute, stroking th hairs on hs chin. "I'll allow it, but you'll have to be put on ice and transported to the gym. Then, we'll free you to use your Dreamer body."

Although Astrid hated the thought of oblivion, even if for a short amount of time, she understood why. If she were conscious during transport, even blindfolded, she could easily learn her way around the facility. "Fine. I'm usually up around five. How's five-thirty?" She stood, hoping he'd get the hint that she was ready to be alone.

Lucien followed her lead and headed for the door. "See you at five-thirty."

After he'd left, loneliness set in again, though not as intense as before. Lucien was right. She needed to let her mind rest as well as her body.

She closed her eyes, and let her consciousness rejoin her sleeping form.

Images of Cyrus and their fight invaded her slumber. He stood over her unconscious body, a maniacal laugh filling the room.

A man with dark hair and light brown eyes appeared in a corner of the room, his face impassive as he watched the scene unfold. He looked somewhat like Lucien, but older.

Cyrus noticed the stranger and sneered. "How does it feel to be helpless?" his voice an evil whisper. "They're all mine."

Astrid awoke with a start. The clock on her bedside table read five-fifteen. She hurried to the closet and changed into workout clothes. This was the first time she'd overslept. Ever.

***

After leaving Astrid, Lucien couldn't sleep. Her face invaded his brain long after he'd left her. Physically, she was his type.

Thick and curvy. Smooth skin the color of polished oak, and eyes that smoldered whether she wanted them to or not. He'd never seen her in makeup, and he liked that. She didn't need it to be gorgeous. Not a single one of the women he'd dated ever let him see them without all the glam makeup, and over-processed, straight hair.

She was a nice, and pleasing change. His wet dream come true. What a waste of what he was sure would be a good time. Sex wasn't a possibility.

He tossed and turned, tempted to try stardust, the sedative his sister used when she needed to sleep in a hurry. But he didn't want to need something to sleep, then something else to wake up. Stardust was some powerful shit.

He tried to piece together the connection between Astrid and his family. She was sure her roommate was the key, but that made no sense. As far as they could tell, Dannen had never been on a case that involved his family. And what's the deal on Cyrus blaming Astrid for Dannen's death? If that was his beef with her, why come after them? And why would Cyrus care? Unless...

He shot out of bed and grabbed his cell, pounding in the code to send a signal outside the facility. "Stephen, I need you to pull Dannen's file again. I think we're digging in the wrong place. I want to know about her family."

"Finding out anything on her family is going to be a tall order. Not even the Dreamers themselves usually know who their father is. I can get you the mother, that's about it."

"Do it." Lucien's adrenalin wouldn't let him sleep. He looked at the digital rendering of Cyrus. "Who are you?"

CHAPTER 4

Lucien sat in the middle of a mat at the end of the floor of the massive gym, tugging at a stray string.

Somiar straddled the weight bench a few feet away. "Looks like your girl's a little late."

He jerked his head up and gave her a withering look. "She's not my girl."

Somiar narrowed her eyes at him. "What's got you so uptight, little brother? The day has just started. A little early to have your drawers in a bunch."

"Have you not been paying attention? Someone is trying to kill us. Again."

"Listen, I'm just as pissed as you are that we have targets on our backs. Again. But Malachi and I have kids to worry about. If anyone, and I mean *anyone* even thinks about harming them, I'll cut out their insides and feed it to them."

"How charming." Lucien stood and stretched. "What do you think of Astrid? Her story seem legit to you?"

"I don't know. Could be. She has to be a seasoned Dreamer. From what I learned from mom, not all Dreamers know the rules of leaving the life unless they've earned a rank high enough to be a Legacy member. Before that point, they haven't put in enough work to even consider getting out. And she couldn't have taken the oath of the Legacy, otherwise she'd have been dead a long time ago. Still, she'd have to be a dumb ass seasoned member to think the Legacy isn't keeping tabs on her."

"Wait one fucking minute," Lucien said. "Are you trying to tell me we may have a member of the freaking Legacy with us?"

Somiar pressed her lips, then huffed. "Lucien, I swear if you don't read Lily's diary, I'm going to skin you alive. There are never more than twelve Legacy members. Membership is passed from mother to daughter unless the Legacy member has no heir. Once you've joined the Legacy, you're bound to them for life. There is no out. Seasoned Dreamers, however, have two ways out. Death, or earn their way out. That would mean doing a job that would guarantee the safety of the Legacy. That could mean killing us." She waved a hand at them both. "Or doing a job so big, you could buy your way out."

She did a couple of squats. "Mom knows of two Dreamers who've achieved that status, and both of them involved the assassination of high-profile clients."

At Lucien's raised brow, she continued. "Think politics and mysteries. And remember, we can trace our heritage back to the 1500s. That's over five hundred years of crap to choose from. What kind of shit happened in five hundred years do you think was worth letting a Dreamer walk?"

"So, what are you trying to say? We've got some kind of super assassin on our hands?" Lucien couldn't believe Astrid could be that vicious. He couldn't imagine her as a cold-blooded killer. But, as a Dreamer, that was her job.

"In case you haven't noticed, she's not dead, so she had to have earned her way out. I'll bet she's killed some pretty important marks. Such an accomplishment before the ripe old age of thirty-six."

"Not exactly true, Somiar." Astrid strolled through the open double doors flanked by two guards.

Lucien tried not to stare. The orange sweat suit she wore was a tad too big. She sported a white tank top and tied the jacket around her waist. Her coarse, black hair had been tamed into a French braid hanging between her shoulder blades. Even dressed for a workout she managed to be sexy as hell.

"Your mother has some outdated information. I'll explain later. Sorry I overslept." She shrugged. "Weird dreams."

Lucien raised a brow. "Did they help?"

"No. Wish they did." She rubbed her hands together and turned to Somiar. "Under the circumstances, nice to see you again, seems a little stupid."

"Don't worry about formalities right now," Somiar returned. "I'm looking forward to this. My mother is the only Dreamer I have to spar with and I know she takes it easy on me. After Monica tried to kill me, I need a hardened partner."

"Ok, but remember, you asked for it. Where do I leave my body?"

Lucien pointed to the mat he'd vacated earlier. "Over there."

Astrid laid down to meditate. Within minutes, she was strolling back in through the gym door dressed in a black tank top, black leggings, and gym shoes. Her hair was blond and cropped close to her head. She grinned. "I never have long hair when sparring, or going after a mark. Hair pulling is a bitch move, but people still do it."

"Hmm." Somiar tapped a fingertip to her bottom lip. "That's a good idea." She chuckled, "The short hair, not the bitch move."

"Okay ladies," Lucien interjected, "Center of the floor please." He strutted over to the benches lining the wall where he noticed Malachi coming in to sit.

"Thought I'd come and see what our newest guest was made of." Malachi twisted his Catcher ring, a habit he had when he was on high alert.

Lucien narrowed his eyes and pressed his lips into a thin line. He was tired of Malachi and Stephen treating him like a rookie.

"So, you're not here to make sure I don't fuck up my first lead assignment?"

Malachi seemed to ignore Lucien's irritated tone. "Not at all. This will be the first time Somiar has fought another Dreamer since that disaster with Monica. I want to see how far she's come."

"Just make sure you keep your distance from the two of them. We don't need your ring glowing."

Malachi turned to Lucien, an annoyed glint in his eye. "Not all of us are gifted with identifying Dreamers without the benefit of a ring."

"Keep that under your hat. I haven't told her about it and she doesn't need to know. We need to keep our element of surprise."

"Excuse us," Somiar called from the center of the room, "are we going to do this, or are y'all going to yap all morning?"

Lucien held his thumbs up then blew two short blasts into his whistle.

***

Somiar was the first to move. She jumped over Astrid's head.

Astrid leaped up and grabbed her around the waist, yanking her down, stopping short of slamming her back over her knee. Instead, she permitted her to land on the padded gym floor.

Astrid circled, making no move to help Somiar up. "I know you said not to take it easy on you, but I don't think you want to know the pain of a broken back."

Somiar hopped to her feet. "Gee, thanks."

Astrid lunged at her, her eyes widening when Somiar punched her in the throat. She immediately healed herself. "Damn, girl, you ain't playing, are you?"

The two women went after each other in earnest. Giving as well as they got. Astrid was the better fighter, but Somiar held her own.

Lucien winced when Astrid flipped Somiar over her shoulder, slamming her on her back, dislocating her shoulder. He cast Malachi a sidelong glance, wondering how he was handling seeing his wife take such a beating.

Somiar healed and attempted to get up, shaking off the injury.

Astrid took advantage of the pause and kicked her feet out from under her. "Never pause, it can get you killed." She straddled her chest, knee in Somiar's shoulder. Although Astrid could feel the bone in her clavicle give under the pressure, she continued to press. "You said not to go easy on you."

Suddenly, Somiar's eyes went stark white.

"What the fuck!" Astrid attempted to scramble off her, but Somiar grabbed her by the throat, flipped her over, and slammed her on her back.

Astrid gazed up at her opponent with stunned eyes. Somiar's eyes were back to normal, a hardened gleam in them. She punched Astrid in the face. "That's for dislocating my shoulder." She punched her again. "That's for the broken bone." And again. "That's because I don't want to take it easy on *you*." Her lips spread in a satisfied grin at the mess she'd made of Astrid's face.

Lucien blew his whistle.

Somiar extended her hand to Astrid to helped her up, then turned to Lucien. "Thanks, little brother."

Lucien smiled. "I was tired of seeing you get your ass handed to you."

"What the hell was that?" Astrid demanded, her face fully healed.

"Little trick between siblings." Lucien offered. "I can see through her eyes when I want. Only problem is it leaves her blind and unable to heal."

Malachi interrupted. "Zip it, Lucien. We still don't know enough about her to be telling secrets."

"Who's she going to tell? She's here, and not going anywhere without us. Besides, she doesn't know where *here* is."

"Um, excuse me. I'm still in the room," Astrid said, clearly annoyed.

Lucien grinned. "Don't mind my brother-in-law. He can be a bit of a prick sometimes."

Silence hung in the air before Lucien cleared his throat. "Time for you to return to your body. Breakfast in an hour."

***

Astrid attacked her breakfast with relish. A small mountain of scrambled eggs, fruit, and toast. Sparring always left her famished, even if she wasn't using her physical body. She would do a double workout if it were permitted later. She didn't notice the rest of the occupants staring at her until she stopped eating long enough to sip her coffee.

"What did you mean when you told Somiar our mother had outdated information?" Lucien asked.

"Those are no longer the only ways to leave the life." Astrid sat back to fiddle with her napkin. "When my mother died, I was supposed to take her place when I came of age. Since that didn't happen, I owe the Legacy an heir. When I have a child, they will expect me to hand her over for training."

Somiar narrowed her eyes. "So, they're short a member. How do we know you're not number twelve?"

"You don't, and there's nothing I can do to convince you." Astrid picked up her glass and guzzled her orange juice. "Actually, there are thirteen Legacy members. Twelve members plus the head. When I didn't take my place as a Legacy, the daughter of another member was elevated. Then, not long after your mother died, another daughter was elevated, then the vote for head was conducted."

"I told you that bitch wasn't my mother," Somiar spat. "Leila is my mother."

Astrid shot Somiar a sidelong glance. "I'm sorry if my saying that upsets you, but as I said, the world, including me, knew Monica as your mother."

Somiar's expression remained hard and unforgiving. "What kind of woman are you? Why would you promise them your child?"

"Because I never plan to have one. You're not naïve. You know good and damned well it would be expected whether I retired or not."

Somiar sighed. "I know. That's one reason my mother kept me a secret. Too bad she let a psycho bitch raise me."

Malachi put a hand on his wife's shoulder. "You know that wasn't her intention. She thought Monica would do right by you."

"Yeah, that worked really well, didn't it," Somiar bit out.

"Our family drama isn't why we're here," Lucien interrupted.

"Yes, it is," Astrid said. "I just don't know how I got added to the mix."

Chimes came from a screen mounted on the wall across the room. Malachi pressed a button on the table, and Stephen and Leila's image appeared.

Leila was still as stone; hell in her eyes. If looks could kill, Astrid would be dead a hundred times over.

Wonder what the hell's eating her.

Without preamble, Stephen cast Astrid a pointed look. "You seem to be very good at your job, young lady. All those years as a hired killer for the Legacy, never photographed nor any hint of your Dreamer identity. That means we have only your word to go on." His hand brushed the gun holstered at his waist. You'd better be on the up and up. Your ass depends on it."

Astrid stood, and stalked closer to the monitor, wishing she could reach through the screen and bitch slap that arrogant bastard. "I *am* good at my job. And you can drop the attempt at intimidation." She flashed an unfriendly smile. "That shit doesn't work on me."

Lucien stepped between the two. "When y'all are done trying to decide who's got bigger balls, can we finish trying to solve the problem at hand?"

"Course we can." Astrid hoped she sounded as casual as she tried. "My balls are bigger. Next question."

Lucien chuckled. "Okay. Now that that's out of the way, I'm hoping Stephen has some information for us."

Stephen's resentful glare never wavered. "I do. Your friend, Dannen, was responsible for the death of several people. She's also responsible for a few assassinations that weren't sanctioned by the Legacy. She wasn't as careful as you were while on assignment. I think she got too comfortable as a Dreamer.

"She was photographed by security cameras, and bystanders. Looks like the Legacy was getting tired of cleaning up after her. The Catcher who killed her gave a description of what she looked like while dreaming." Stephen and Leila's image was replaced with several photos.

Astrid gazed at the images of her friend in her Dreamer body, zeroing in on one. Dannen was on a dance floor in a crowded room. A man was pressed against her almost as tight as the black silk catsuit she wore. Her auburn braids hung down to her waist, white gold chains entwined in them, a bejeweled star headband finished the look. Her normally light skin, a smooth mahogany, her eyes a shocking blue.

Astrid knew the look well. She'd helped Dannen pick it out. The headband was the perfect way to camouflage her throwing stars. She'd cautioned Dannen against the blue eyes and extra-long hair. It would make her stand out way too much.

"That was the look Dannen used when she was out for a good time, not on assignment." Astrid pointed at the picture. "She didn't intend to kill anyone that night. She's having fun, not hunting."

"No, according to our radar, there were no deaths to make our antennae go up. But the next night," Stephen enlarged one photo, "We got this one."

Astrid studied the photo. It was Dannen alright. Only this time, she looked the way she always did. Hair shaved close to her scalp on one side and in back, long black hair streaked with blond covering one eye on the other. She wore black jeans with holes in the knees and thigh and a black t-shirt that read, 'Pretend you don't see me' across the front in small white letters. She couldn't make out her eye color.

"Anyone notice the background?" Lucien's voice sounded tense behind her.

Malachi absently stroked his chin. "That's Richard's old house."

Somiar's eyes narrowed. "I hope you're not talking about the Richard I think you are."

Malachi nodded. "I am."

Lucien stepped up to Astrid, coming face to face with her. "Would you a care to explain why your friend is in front of my father's property?"

Astrid licked suddenly dry lips. She wanted to give them the answers to their questions, but she couldn't. She was just as surprised as they were. "I don't know. Dannen never mentioned your family. Besides, is there a law against walking down the street? Maybe she was passing by."

"In a residential neighborhood way outside her zip code. In the middle of the night. Using her Dreamer body?" Lucien asked.

"This isn't her Dreamer body," Astrid argued.

"Yes, it is." Lucien pointed out the caption at the bottom of the photo. "It's a secure neighborhood. There are cameras all over that street. The only blind spot is on that corner. She was never picked up again. In order to disappear without being seen, she had to have been dreaming. And she would have to know where the blind spot is. Why would she be there?"

"You're asking me questions I don't have answers to. And how do I know these pictures aren't fake? I'm sure tactics like this aren't beneath you. Neighborhood cameras can't get such good detail at night."

"The original was fuzzy, but we have equipment to clear it up. Facial recognition shows it's Dannen. A few changes to her Dreamer hair and body here and there, but her face is the same." Stephen tossed a sarcastic smile Astrid's way. "Now are you going to answer my questions, or persist on trying to be the interrogator?"

A chill crept down Astrid's neck. None of this made sense. "I have no idea why she was there. She didn't even know him. I know it's a weird coincidence, but just because she walked down his street once..."

"No." Leila interrupted. "Take a look at some of the other photos. She was caught several times at his gravesite, day, and night. Sometimes in her physical body, sometimes her Dreamer body. One of the mausoleum cameras has his grave in range. Several videos show her rounding corners and disappearing once out of sight."

"What have you got on her mother?" Lucien asked.

"That's where the plot thickens." Stephen steepled his fingers. "Her mother went by the name Calypso. She was a seasoned Dreamer who did small hit jobs for the Legacy. Never assigned a Catcher or a high profile mark. Gun for hire through and through."

Astrid leaned back in her chair. "That didn't make her very popular with the Dreamers who did the important jobs."

Lucien drew his brows together in a frown. "Why not? A Dreamer is a Dreamer. If the Legacy sanctioned her kills, why would it matter who the prey was?"

Somiar laughed. "Because even Dreamers have their cliques and hierarchy. Monica told me that some Dreamers did what she described as pro-bono work. Pedophiles and rapists who get off on a technicality. Thieves, or rich assholes other rich assholes wanted out of the way, willing to pay millions to get what they wanted. Of course, they know nothing of Dreamers or the Legacy. I don't know how the deal is done or money exchanged."

"What does that have to do with Calypso?" Lucien seemed to be losing patience with the conversation.

Astrid turned to face him. "The common assassin Dreamers are low on the totem pole. They're above the rookies, but below the elite high-profile and Catcher assassins. Although they get paid very well, they're paid much less."

"You're kidding me." A smile tugged at Lucien's lips. "Some of the Dreamers are snobs?" A robust laugh burst from his lips. "Who knew? Mean-girl Dreamers."

"That's not funny," Astrid snapped. "Dannen was only two when her mother died and she regretted never being raised or trained by her. She was raised by the Legacy, and to them, the daughter of a low-level Dreamer is nothing more than an expendable asset until proven worthy to be more. It wasn't a secret that she was ashamed of her mom. She made it her mission not to be like her." Astrid hung her head. "Problem was, it made her reckless. Always felt like she had something to prove because of her mother's status."

Lucien sobered. "I'm sorry. I don't mean to mock the dead. Never a good look, whether you liked them or not." He motioned to Stephen. "Anything else?"

Stephen tossed Lucien a level look. "Just one. Calypso's last mark was the owner of a convenience store in what's now condos in the Fourth Ward. He was the only holdout. She planned to make the hit look like a robbery. The store owner had a young man who worked for him part time. When she tried to hold up the store, he caught her in the act, and got the gun the owner kept in the back office. Shot her in the chest and killed her."

Stephen paused and glanced at Leila.

Leila gave a slight nod and took his hand in hers.

Stephen returned his attention to Lucien. "The man who killed her was Richard Drake."

Chapter 5

Lucien's heart pounded in his ears. "What're you talking about? You mean dad killed Dannen's mother?"

"Yes." Stephen ran a hand over his head. He directed his gaze to Malachi. "I remember that day. Richard and I were partners, and he spent quite a bit of his spare time working in the store. There was a lot of trouble in that part of the ward. Richard wanted to help the people struggling to hold on to their property, so he befriended the store owner, and told the man he needed the work. We didn't know the Legacy was involved."

Lucien's brows drew together. "Dad never mentioned any of this to me."

"That's because he died before he could start your training. You didn't even know he was a Catcher until we had to save your ass six years ago."

"True. I suppose dad got off because if was self-defense."

Stephen shook his head. "No. The store owner got off because it was self- defense."

"What?" Lucien pressed his lips together in a perplexed frown.

"Richard's ring glowed the moment he got near the body. She was a Dreamer. Do you really think we would let police have her body?"

Astrid grimaced. "Oh, my stars, I just remembered. Cyrus wore a Catcher's ring."

"What? Are you sure?" Stephen up his hand. "He had one of these?"

Astrid turned away in disgust. "Of course, I'm sure. Those damned things have gotten my ass in more tight spots than a virgin on her wedding day."

Lucien gave her a sidelong glance. "Um, okay."

"Seriously." Astrid sucked on her lower lip. "What are we missing? A *man* claims to be a Dreamer, even though Dreamers are women. He wears a Catcher's ring, but a Dreamer body can't come near those things without setting them off, and he has powers that neither Dreamers nor Catchers possess. What the hell are we missing?"

Lucien collapsed in a chair. "The only thing I can figure is he's pretending to be a Dreamer."

"But why? And why wear a Catcher's ring? And what does he have to do with Dannen and your family?" Astrid sat down and leaned her head back against the chair, closing her eyes.

Lucien surveyed her for a moment trying to get a read on her. He couldn't figure her out. She seemed sincere. But what if she wasn't?

He smiled when he heard the 'ABC song' ring tone from Somiar's phone.

"The children are up," Somiar announced. She took Malachi's hand and headed to the door. "This is important, but our children are more so. Besides, we promised to have tea with them and their imaginary friend."

Malachi chuckled. "According to Ruby, Bubba makes really good tea."

Lucien laughed. "That's one heck of a name for an imaginary friend." He waved a hand. "Ya'll go on. I'm going to try to sift through more of this. Kiss my niece and nephews for me."

Stephen inclined his head toward Astrid. "What about her?"

"Care to put in some more time on this?" Lucien asked.

Astrid nodded. "It's not like I have something better to do."

"Stephen, send the pics. We're gonna spend more time on them. We'll let you know if we find anything."

"Way ahead of you. They're on the way to your laptop and copies should be coming through the printer now."

Lucien pulled photos from the printer and sifted through them along with reports of Dannen. He stopped at one and held it up. "You're in this one."

Astrid took the photo and smiled. She and Dannen were in a restaurant. They sat at a table, holding up a glass of champagne in a toast. "I remember this. Our first night out without the supervision of the Legacy. Sort of like a graduation. We were to move into our apartment the next day."

"We knew the two of you were roommates. The Catchers checked you out when they noticed you spent a lot of time together, but they never could get anything on you. They figured you were just an ordinary girl. It's not uncommon for Dreamers to have friends that have nothing to do with the life."

"True. Dannen's mother left her enough to live on for the rest of her life, as did my mine. Even though we could afford to live on our own, we'd been best friends for as long as I can remember. Moving in together seemed like the natural thing to do."

Lucien studied her for a moment. "Where are your parents?"

"You should know. You had me checked out."

"All we know is the story we were supposed to find. Your mother was the founder and CEO of a very lucrative tech company, and your father died in a fire before you were born. I'm asking for the real story, not the one used to hide your identity."

Astrid stood and went to the bar. Pouring herself a glass of water, she kept her back to him. "My mother was a Legacy. She died eleven years ago, and I sold off the company to a Legacy member. I know who my father is, but I've never met him. He was a lowlife, and of course, doesn't know about me. She left a diary with the Legacy and it was passed down to me."

"You mean that's not against the rules?"

"No. And notice I said she left the diary to the Legacy members. By the time I got it, there's no telling what they took out or put in."

Lucien twisted his lips in distaste. "I guess they learned from my family to monitor what's told to those left behind. Had they gotten to my ancestor's diaries before we did, we would've never known the truth of our heritage."

"I guess so. Some of us have diaries, but I think they're a waste of time. We know we don't have a long life expectancy, considering our jobs. Falling in love isn't recommended, but it happens. As long as it doesn't interfere with missions, we can do whatever we want in our personal lives. Your mom crossed the line when she married a Catcher." Astrid cocked her head and smirked. "Are all Catchers this clueless about us?"

Lucien traced a pattern on the table. "It's not like Dreamers and Catchers sit down for friendly conversations. Even though Somiar is a Dreamer, she wasn't brought up in the life, and Leila, as you say, has some outdated intel. You're the only one we've come across willing to give us any current information."

Astrid bit her lip. "That's because we have a shared enemy. You know, the enemy of my enemy saying. Besides, after learning the story of your sister and Malachi, I'm more on the 'can't we all get along' train."

Lucien continued to contemplate her. The only Dreamers he trusted were Somiar and Leila. Astrid was raised in the way of the Dreamers. Until he was absolutely sure of her, she would be kept on a short leash.

After hours of staring at pictures and finding nothing, Astrid stretched, and rubbed her temples. "This is going nowhere." She looked to Lucien. "I was wondering if I could use the gym for a couple of extra hours. My Dreamer body got a great workout this morning, but my physical body, not so much."

"Sure, you can. I work out at five every evening. It's intense, but it helps me sleep."

"Seriously?" Astrid knitted her brows. "I'm usually hyped up after a workout."

"That's why I start so early. You'll see. Couple that with a good meal and a hot tub soak before bed."

"Doesn't sound like a bad idea. The hot tub in my bathroom looks like heaven." She glanced around the room. "How much time do you spend here?"

"Not much. Since I've been out of training, most of my time is spent up top."

"You mean we're underground?"

Lucien kept his voice neutral. "Isn't the Legacy?"

"I don't know. Only Legacy members are in on how and where they meet, and I lost interest in becoming Legacy long ago."

She rubbed the back of her neck and rolled her shoulders. "Once mom died, I was trained by various high-level Dreamers. After hearing the story of your family, I decided to leave. I want to see peace. The

Dreamers and Legacy have done some good, but doing the wrong thing for the right reasons is still the wrong thing. And the bad seriously outweighs the good."

Lucien rubbed his chin, not sure if he believed her. "Let's take a walk. I need to stretch my legs." Without giving her a chance to answer, he strode to the door. Two guards stepped in line to follow, but Lucien held up a hand. "I got it guys."

Astrid took in the stark white hallway. They made several turns, each hall identical. "You guys need a decorator," Astrid mused.

"Nah. It looks exactly the way we want it to. I was here a couple of months before I learned my way around." He stopped at a door that blended into the wall.

When the door slid open, warm, humid air curled the hairs that had come free from her braid. Small trees and plants filled the room. "What's this?"

"Modeled after the Amazon. There's one just like it in the Botanical Gardens downtown, only they have live birds. I like to go there for a little peace and quiet sometimes." Lucien entered the room, a smile lighting up his face. "It's nice to have it here too."

Astrid took a seat on a small bench next to a bush boasting bright red flowers. "Yes, I've been there before. Got one hell of a mosquito bite. I looked like I had two elbows for three days."

He smiled, "No mosquitos here." Taking the empty spot by her side, he breathed in the floral scented air. "Don't you have a place to go when you want to be alone with your thoughts?"

"Don't need it. I live alone." She motioned to the camera in the corner, "How are you alone with your thoughts when someone is watching?"

He shrugged. "I guess I've learned to ignore it."

Astrid looked up at him. "It's nice to get away from the crazy. For the last couple of days, my life has been taken over by the crazy."

His lips stretched to a thin line. "For the last few *years* my life has been taken over by the crazy." Their gazes locked.

Every inch of him wanted to kiss her. He kept telling himself it was a bad idea, but his body didn't listen, and he leaned in.

Her eyes fluttered closed.

His lips softly brushed hers. When she didn't back away, he went deeper, his tongue meeting hers.

She ran her hand up his back, cradling he back of his neck, then pulled away. "I can't do this." She jumped from the bench. "I need to go."

"What's wrong?" Lucien stood next to her and gently touched her arm.

"I can't ignore the fact that we have an audience, and we both know this is not a normal situation." She went to stand in front of the door. "I want to go. Now."

Lucien opened the door and stepped aside to let her pass, then glared at the camera, holding up a middle finger. "Thanks for nothing, assholes."

CHAPTER 6

Astrid glanced at the clock for what seemed like a million times. Dressed and ready for the past two hours, she drummed her fingers on the table, and stared at the door like a puppy waiting for its owner to come home. She'd been invited to join the family for lunch, but after letting Lucien kiss her, she wasn't ready to face him. Taking the meal in her room seemed to be the safest thing to do. Now it felt like the walls were closing in on her.

Getting all that excess adrenaline and frustration out at the gym was just what she needed. Besides, she knew they were being gracious by allowing her to her opt out of the past meal. She was pretty sure she wouldn't be given an option later. They believed she had the answers to all their questions, and she wasn't sure she didn't.

She sprang from her chair when her door opened, raring to go, deflated when the guard appeared.

Good night! This man was a mountain of muscle. He towered over her as if she were a child and she was five-nine. He wasn't the same guard she'd had earlier. Her guards seemed to change at regular intervals.

"Turn and face the wall, please." His soft voice didn't fit his frame.

Astrid studied him for a moment, rooted to the spot, still stunned by his appearance.

"Ma'am, please turn around and face the wall," he repeated.

She complied with a grimace. "Why do you call me ma'am? I can't be that much older than you."

"You're not. You got me beat by three years. But I call all women ma'am, and men, sir. I was raised in a military family. It's our way."

Her eyes widened. "How do you know how old I am?"

"I read it in your file. Since part of my job is guarding you, it's my business to know some things about you." He moved to stand next to her and held up a blindfold and headphones. "These are going to be used for transport to the gym." He tossed them on a table. "Please put your hands next to the rings on the wall."

For the first time, she noticed the small metal rings bolted into the wall by the bathroom. She placed her hands beside them and fought the urge to engage the mountain in a fight when he pulled out metal shackles. He attached one to each of her wrists, then to the wall. A thin iron rod was added to the wrist brace portion of the shackles. He placed the blindfold over her eyes, then headphones, playing loud static.

She felt the pressure from the shackles being released from the wall, her hands weighed down by the bar. "Is all of this really necessary?"

The static ceased from the headphones, and her escort's voice came through. "Yes ma'am. Since you're being transported conscious, we have to take extra precautions. We can skip this if you'd rather be pinned."

Wow. This is overkill. Where in the hell do they think I'm going to go?

It took a moment for her to realize this was nothing more than a show of dominance. They wanted her to know they were in charge.

The static resumed. Astrid tried to block it out. The warmth of a hand at her elbow made her turn her head toward the body next to her.

They took several steps before she was loaded into what she assumed was some kind of cart. The Dreamer assassin in her couldn't help but count the steps and amount of time she was in motion. She strained to hear through the static in her ears, but no background noise came through.

The Catchers were smarter than she'd been led to believe. She was constantly getting on and off some form of motorized transportation, and walking for what seemed a random number of steps.

Finally, she was ushered forward. The shackles, blindfold, and headphones removed. She was in a large room, full of exercise equipment. It reminded her of the gym she went to in her neighborhood.

Lucien entered at the other end of the room, looking devilishly handosme in his workout clothes. "Hi there, hope you haven't been waiting long."

"This isn't the gym we were in this morning." She could think of nothing else to say.

He pursed his lips in a suppressed smile and raised a brow. "I know. You said you wanted to work out, not spar."

"Yeah, right. How many gyms are here?"

"Enough."

Ignoring the vague answer, she mounted a piece of equipment to do a quick warm up, before working out in earnest.

She didn't realize how much she pushed herself until her muscles started screaming in protest. Trying to ease the weight down on the arm machine, she realized there was no way to gracefully let it rest to the other weights. Her muscles trembled with the effort before she let it drop, the loud clang breaking the rhythmic sound of the machine Lucien was using.

Ignoring him when he gazed her way, she closed her eyes and crossed her arms in front of her trying to work the kinks out of her shoulders.

Lucien grinned. "When you work hard, you should always give yourself a reward."

She looked up at him as he pushed a button on the wall.

Two identical women strode into the room carrying massage tables. Tall as Amazons, muscles gently defined, they could give Gal Gadot a run for her money, in beauty and grace. They went about setting up their tables without so much as a word.

Lucien shrugged. "You were working those machines like Satan himself was coaching you. I figured you were going to be in knots. These ladies have magic hands."

Astrid stared longingly at the tables. "You don't know how good that sounds right now."

"Yes, I do." Lucien grinned. "Been there, done that."

Two folding screens were placed a few feet from the tables.

Lucien jerked a thumb at one of them. "You can go back there to change."

Astrid did a double take. "Wait. You're getting one too?"

"Of course. I couldn't let you show me up." He stretched his arms over his head. "I had to keep up."

He poured a glass of cucumber-lemon water from the dispenser near the door and took a sip before disappearing behind the screen.

It took very little time before he reappeared in a bathrobe.

The two masseuses turned their backs.

"Are you in or out? Either way, I'm dropping this robe and getting a massage. Peppermint and Patty are the best in the business."

Astrid twisted her lips. "Are you serious?"

"Don't blame me." Lucien laughed. "That's the name their momma gave them."

It was the women's turn to laugh. "He's telling the truth. Our parents had a weird sense of humor. We thought about changing our names, but I grew to like mine. It's unique." The woman had a lyrical, friendly voice.

"I never liked mine," the other exclaimed. "Patty is not a name you want to grow up with. People always lengthen my name to Patricia. I've been hamburger patty, rice patty, crabby patty. Thankfully, when we were growing up, sis would change places with me occasionally. She dealt out a lot of ass whippings on my behalf."

Astrid chuckled. "I was starting to think you two didn't speak."

"We speak when we have something to say," said Patty. There was a hint of a smile in her tone.

"Far be it from me to decline a couple's massage from Peppermint-Patty." She ducked behind the screen hoping Lucien didn't notice her slip referring to themselves as a couple.

When she emerged, he was already face down on the table.

Her masseuse kept her back to her while she laid down and pulled the sheet over her waist. Astrid tried to keep her mind off the fact that Lucien was a couple of feet away, nude.

Soft hands massaged her scalp, then slowly slid to her neck, then her shoulders.

Her lids felt heavy. She struggled to remain awake, unease gripping her mind like a vise. Why was she so sleepy? This shouldn't be happening.

She tried to get off the table, but her body wouldn't cooperate. She wanted to speak in protest, but couldn't form the words. Why would he drug her? What were they going to do? She fought with all her might to stay awake, but it was futile.

Astrid's eyes snapped open. She was in her house. She watched herself thumb through her mail, like she had done a thousand times. Although she knew what was coming next, she still didn't want to face it.

An attempt to summon her Dreamer body proved useless. The gym must be protected from her Dreamer powers. She raked a nail down her arm, hoping the pain would wake her up, but the scratches instantly healed. Oh, crap. She *was* in her Dreamer body.

She ran her fingers across her forehead, gazing at the moisture on her fingers. This shouldn't be happening. Who sweats in a dream? "What the fuck is going on," she yelled. Her outcry went unanswered.

"Dreamer." A masculine, disembodied voice softly drew the word out.

Her spine stiffened when she observed her doppelganger respond to the whisper. The eeriness of the scene sent a chill all over her body.

Out of nowhere, Cyrus was in her living room.

Lucien appeared at her side. He stared in wide-eyed disbelief at her, and the scene playing out in front of him. "What the hell is going on?"

"You tell me. Why did you drug me? I would have told you whatever you wanted to know." She clenched her jaw, trying to calm the annoying twitch at her temple. "What is this? Some kind of truth serum the Catchers have concocted? Not even my Dreamer body can leave the confines of this circus."

"I don't know what the hell you're talking a...whoa!" He stopped to watch her kick the shit out of Cyrus, then deliver a vicious blow to the man's nuts. He winced, his hand covering his own groin. "That had to hurt." He gasped when the man didn't even flinch.

"Yeah, my sentiments exactly." Astrid studied the fight, waiting for Lucien's reaction when Cyrus healed himself.

"What the hell?" Lucien followed her as she circled the scene. "What's going on with this guy?"

His voice faded into the background as she focused on the mayhem playing out in front of them.

She reigned in her emotions, as she was taught during her training, and let her analytical mind take over. *This is over. This is the past. Pay attention.* She watched in detached curiosity when he punched her in the face.

There has to be something, some clue to as to who Cyrus is.

The man from her previous dream appeared next to her and whispered in her ear. "Look closely."

Astrid gazed into the man's eyes. Time seemed to stop. Slowly, she turned from him to Cyrus, focusing on his face. Something familiar. She strained to put her finger on it.

Lucien, started toward them. "Dad?"

The man gazed at Lucien, smiled, then disappeared.

Astrid was jolted out of her trance and time resumed its normal speed. "Whatever you gave me, you need to reverse it. Right now."

"For the last time I didn't-"

Astrid's eyes fluttered open before Lucien could finish the sentence. She jumped off the massage table and pulled the sheet up to cover herself.

"Is everything okay?" The masseuse jumped back.

"What did you do to me?" Astrid narrowed her eyes at Patty and backed away from the table. Her gaze strayed to where Lucien lay unmoving, Peppermint roughly shaking his shoulder, trying to wake him.

"I didn't do anything. I asked you to turn over, and you jumped up." Her hand was poised at her waist.

Astrid wasn't sure what weapon was concealed there, but if it was a gun, she knew she couldn't dodge a bullet. Her heart thumped and her body went rigid, waiting for whatever was coming. She damned herself for letting herself get even a little comfortable here.

Lucien stirred and took a leisurely stretch before sitting up. Noting the obvious tension in the room, he furrowed his brow. "Stand down, ladies." Keeping the sheet around his waist, he stood to face Astrid. Without turning, he spoke to the twins. "I think Astrid and I need a moment alone."

"You sure?" Peppermint asked.

"Yes, please." Lucien's gaze never left Astrid.

Once the ladies left the room, Astrid turned a frosty gaze to Lucien. "Let me guess. Even the massage therapists are packing here?"

"Of course. Everyone working here can defend themselves." He turned and dropped the sheet, giving her a full view of his bare ass, and put on his bathrobe, tying it at the waist. Turning back to face her, his lips spread in a lazy smile. "I find it laughable you'd think otherwise."

She fought the heat creeping up her cheeks. "I don't find any of your fun-house tricks funny at all. What kind of sick games are ya'll playing?"

He ignored her discomfort and continued. "I fell asleep on the table. I told you the ladies are good at their jobs." He poured two large glasses of water and gave her one. "Would have been more relaxing had it not been for the fucked-up dream I had."

"You had a fucked-up dream?" She cast him a level stare. Still unsure of his motives, she decided to go along and see where this yellow brick road was going. "Must be contagious. So did I. There are some things I remember about that night in my apartment. Something about Cyrus is familiar."

Taking a sip from his glass, he arched a brow. "Care to elaborate?"

"It didn't hit me until my dream. When I met Cyrus at my restaurant, there was something about the way he looked at me. I noticed his Catcher's ring, but didn't realize it was a fake until we fought."

Lucien twisted his lips, clearly unimpressed. "Of course it was. Had it been real, and he was a Dreamer as he claimed, it would have been glowing when you fought. Anything else?"

Astrid wasn't sure what she was looking for. "Yeah. I mean, it was a dream. Had all the weird elements."

"What weird elements?"

"Some strange dude who looked like an older version of you showed up again."

That seemed to get his attention. "What do you mean, again?"

"I saw him once before in a dream. Cyrus seemed to have it in for him. I remember Cyrus telling him, 'you can't save them,' or something along those lines."

Lucien went to the monitor at the end of the room and pulled up a picture. "Is this him?"

Astrid's eyes widened. "Yes. How did you know?"

"That's my father. Astrid, we had the same dream."

"How is that possible? You sure we weren't drugged or something?" Her heart pounded.

What the heck was going on? How in the hell was she dreaming about a man she'd never met? She squeezed her eyes shut trying to concentrate. She had to have seen him before. And what the hell is it about Cyrus's face that bugged her?

Lucien ignored her and headed back behind the changing screen. When he emerged, fully dressed in his workout clothes, he pulled out his phone. "Family conference, now."

Malachi's voice came over the line. "Mind if we do this in the main quarters? Somiar and I are trying to keep the kids close. They keep telling us their imaginary friend wants us to stay with them. They won't go to sleep because they're afraid we'll leave."

"Fine. We just had some strange shit happen down here. Astrid and I are on our way."

CHAPTER 7

Astrid settled in on an oversized bean bag chair, legs curled under her, surrounded by various memebers of Lucien's family.

His five-year-old niece and two nephews, played in a corner of the room busily chatting, occasionally pausing to gaze at a space in the center of their small circle.

Somiar and Malachi watched over them.

Stephen and Leila, were tapped in via video. Although Stephen wasn't related by blood, he clearly cared for, and loved them all. Especially Leila.

How she wished she could have grown up in a family like this. Sure, she was raised by her mother in her early years, but the Dreamers were her sisters, the Legacy, her guardians. None of them were the touchy, 'I love you' types. Strength, duty, loyalty, control, and a whole lot of violence. Her faux family taught her to survive, made her a rich woman, and turned her into a top-notch killer.

"I'm telling you, man. We had a shared dream." Lucien paced the floor, not able to sit longer than a few seconds before pacing again. "I know the story about the Catcher's vision, but this was so *not* that."

Astrid jerked her head up at his statement. What the hell? Catcher's vision? Maybe it would be best if she left that one alone. The sooner they took care of this Cyrus problem, the sooner she could go back to her nice, not so boring life. She didn't want to think about them deciding to not let her go.

"We had the same dream." Lucien ran his hand over his head. "And let's not ignore the fact that *both* of us fell asleep. It was uncontrollable. I was trying to figure out how she managed to drug me."

"And I was wondering the same thing about you," Astrid added. "I was relaxed, enjoying my massage, and suddenly, no matter how hard I tried, I couldn't keep my eyes open."

Malachi stroked his chin. "And she saw Richard, even though she's never met him?"

"Not just her," Lucien corrected, "I saw him too. When I said his name, he gave me the strangest look. Then disappeared."

"Um...sorry, *not sorry*," Somiar interrupted, her voice dripping with sarcasm. "But how do we know she didn't pull some kind of crap on you? How do you know she didn't slip a little stardust in the massage oil used on you? It was Monica's greatest trick. Topically, that shit will still knock you out cold."

Astrid glared at Somiar. "All of you have been watching me like a hawk since I've been here. How do you suppose I got my hands on stardust?"

Astrid liked Somiar. Her kick-ass attitude was one she could rock with. But right now, she wanted to knock the shit out of her. Sure, the woman had a reason to be suspicious. But logic didn't seem to be her strong suit.

"What would be the point? I suppose I knocked myself out too? And neither Peppermint nor Patty were wearing gloves, but they weren't affected." Astrid jerked her head in Lucien's direction. "How would you explain my manipulating his dreams?" She threw her hands in the air in frustration. "I have no control over another person's subconscious. I couldn't even control my Dreamer body."

Malachi spoke up. "Wait. What do you mean your Dreamer body? You were able to project?"

"Not exactly. I couldn't project shit." Astrid rubbed her temples. "I couldn't interact with the outside world. My Dreamer body was stuck in the dream with Lucien."

Malachi cast a suspicious, sidelong glance. "Something about this reeks. Lucien, are you sure about what you saw? Both of you said you felt like you were drugged. We know Peppermint and Patty didn't do it. They've worked with us for years."

Stephen, unusually quiet, joined in the conversation. "Everyone in this family is in danger." He gestured at Astrid. "The common link is you." He addressed the others in the room. "Think about it. Dreamers have never been able to get into Lucien's house. She shows up on his doorstep, and is not only brought into the house, but the Catcher Station. The only thing we know about her is what she's told us. I'll admit, her story had me reeled in too, but why should we believe anything she has to say? She's a Dreamer."

Leila leaped to her feet and slapped his shoulder. "Wait one fucking minute, you fucking asshole. I'm a Dreamer, Somiar is a Dreamer, my granddaughter is a Dreamer. Are we all suspect too? Maybe Julian and Gideon should put their sister out of her misery. As her brothers, and Catchers, they should have the job."

Astrid could feel the tension from Leila. The monitors almost pulsated with her rage.

"That's not what I meant, and you know it!" Stephen shot back.

"What did you mean?" Astrid asked, her voice soft.

"You were born and raised in the way of Dreamers and the Legacy." Stephen's stony expression never changed. "I think we should put it to a vote."

Lucien went to stand in front of Astrid. "A vote for what?"

"We should put Astrid on ice. At least until we know what's going on," Stephen finished.

Astrid gasped. "But I've done nothing to deserve that. I haven't lied to any of you." Her pulse pounded in her ears. Her palms sweat and she clenched her hands together to stop the trembling. She forced herself to speak though her mouth was bone dry. "On the blood of my mother, everything I've told you is true."

"Your mother was a Legacy member. Her blood means nothing to me." Stephen said with a glacial stare. His tone held fast, despite an irritated Leila sitting next to him.

Astrid's anger turned to rage at his declaration. She darted around Lucien, no longer caring what they did to her. "You self-righteous piece of shit! What makes your life worth so much more than mine?"

Lucien's arm snaked around her waist, holding her in place, his body warm and reassuring against her back.

"What makes your hopes and dreams worth more? Had it not been for a Dreamer, your sorry ass wouldn't even exist. Have you forgotten what you've learned? We all a come from one race." Tears streamed down her face. "One race."

Stephen glanced at the others in the group. "We need to take a vote."

Lucien still held Astrid strong in his embrace. "No, we don't. And I swear, Stephen, if you make one move to have her pinned, I'll find you and beat the shit out of you."

The children stopped their play.

Julien wailed. "Bubba, make them stop!"

Brilliant white light filled the room.

Astrid squinted against the glare.

Lucien's grip around her waist loosened.

Astrid's legs no longer had the strength to keep her upright. She dropped to the floor, but something broke her fall. Her vision cleared long enough for her to see a man. Dark skin, long dreads, and a kind smile.

Astrid summoned the strength to reach out and touch his hair. "I guess Lucien couldn't keep him from killing me. At least an angel came for me." The world went black.

CHAPTER 8

Lucien struggled to open his eyes. His lids felt as if they had a thick paste holding them together. Trying to bring fuzzy shapes into focus, he blinked several times.

Dark, coconut scented hair tickled his nose. Astrid's warm, slender body nestled at his side didn't move, but her soft breathing reassured him. He lay on the floor of the main quarters spooning her.

What the hell happened? The last thing he remembered was challenging Stephen to a fight. His gaze darted to things in his line of vision. He didn't want to make any sudden moves and alert whoever knocked them out. Malachi and Somiar were slumped over in their chairs. Stephen and Leila were still on the monitors, also unconscious.

Astrid stirred against him. She stretched and turned over, snuggling against his chest. When she opened her eyes and saw him, he slowly raised a finger to his lips.

"It's okay, son. We know you're awake." The deep voice was vaguely familiar.

"Like Santa," came Gideon's sing song voice.

Lucien jumped to his feet, bringing Astrid with him, searching for the source of the disembodied voice.

Malachi and Somiar jerked awake, then rushed to their children's side, looking them over, worry marring their features.

Stephen lurched to his feet, taking a protective stance in front of Leila. "Who said that?"

Julien giggled. "Bubba! And he brought some friends. Hello, Bubba's friends."

Gideon waved.

Ruby curtsied. "How do you do?"

"Mal, what the hell is going on?" Lucien asked, backing up.

Malachi took Somiar by the hand and gathered the children behind them. "I don't know. Stephen, did you hear what I heard?"

"Yeah, and we both know what we just heard ain't possible."

Leila caught her breath. "It can't be."

Lucien addressed the children. "Julien, who's Bubba?"

"Our friend." Julien stopped for a moment, head cocked, then nodded. "He said don't be afraid. They're here to help. They want you to stop fighting. You have to help each other."

"Why can't we see Bubba?" Lucien tried to keep his tone conversational.

After a pause, Julien replied. "You can if he wants you to. He wants to make sure you're ready. Don't get scared. He don't want to hurt you."

"Okay, tell Bubba we're ready." Lucien straightened and waited.

"Hello, Son."

Lucien stared at the man who appeared out of thin air. His father looked exactly as he remembered. Thick, black wavy hair. Neatly trimmed thin mustache, muscular build, taller than Lucien. Another man and woman stood slightly behind him.

The man with him was a tall, black man with dreads gathered at the nape of his neck, trailing down his back.

The woman was beautiful, coily light brown hair down to her shoulders.

Lucien stood back, his heart racing in his ears. "Dad," he gasped. "How can this be?'

*****

Richard stepped back to admire his children. His glance went from Lucien to Somiar, the daughter he never knew he had. His jaw involuntarily clenched when he saw Leila. How dare she make that decision for him.

The look she exchanged with Stephen wasn't lost on him. He would deal with her later. Right now, all he wanted to do was go to his children and wrap them in his arms, but knew that would be unwise. After all, he was a dead man.

"What is this?" Stephen roared. "What the hell is going on!" He glared at Astrid. "What kind of sick trick are you playing?"

"Me?" Astrid's eyes widened. "I have no idea who this man is, and unless you're totally stupid, I've been here two days and still don't know where *here* is."

Lucien swallowed, pulling her closer. "Don't you remember? From the dream? This man looks like my father."

Richard tried to keep the sadness from his eyes. His son didn't know him anymore. It'd been years since his death. Thank goodness, Jude was there to keep everyone's emotions in check. The last thing he needed right now was a group of hysterical people with volatile tempers.

Astrid inhaled, her gaze going from Richard, then back to Stephen. "So now you're accusing me of raising the dead?" She raised her hands in resignation. "Are you fucking kidding me?"

Malachi stepped forward and stood in front of Richard. "I hate to interrupt this impromptu séance, family reunion, but where the hell did you come from?"

Richard chuckled. "Mal, good to see you again. "Who, or should I say, *what* I am, is going to take some explaining. Unfortunately, we don't have a lot of time."

He motioned to the man and woman with him. "This is Kalyste." The curly haired woman inclined her head.

Somiar inhaled sharply.

Kalyste cast a reassuring smile her way.

He motioned to his friend with the dreads. "And this is Jude."

Richard tried not to stare at Leila, the love of his life, as she sat there, dumbstruck, clutching the arm of his best friend. "I was able to find you because I know about this Catcher station and its location. Sooner or later, she's going to get the help she needs to find it too."

"Enough of this shit." Stephen glared at Richard. "If you learned to change gender, so be it, but you're still a Dreamer."

"You always were a little bit of a hot-head." Richard raised his hand at eye level. "And a blabber mouth to boot."

Stephen's mouth continued to move, but no sound came out.

"Did someone mute the screen?" Lucien picked up the remote and pushed the buttons.

"Stephen! Are you okay?" Leila placed her palms on Stephen's cheeks. "Can you hear me?" She spoke louder. "Are you hurt? What happened to your voice?"

When Stephen shook his head, she turned back to glare at Richard. "Who are you, really? What do you want? What did you do?"

Richard narrowed his eyes. "Oh, come now Leila. Don't you recognize your own husband?" He spoke between clenched teeth. "I loved you, trusted you, apparently more than you did me. How could you keep me away from my own flesh and blood?"

"My husband is dead. Why are you impersonating him?" Her eyes filled with tears. "Who are you?" she whispered.

Richard grimaced, keeping a leash on his anger. "Just a little trick I learned in my new life. He's going to be fine."

He glared at her, unmoved by her display of emotion. "I hate what you've done to me. Who you've kept from me."

He gazed at Somiar, knowing his longing to go to her was written all over his face, but her expression was one of mild curiosity. He looked into the eyes of a stranger, and so did she.

"Lucky for you, I'm forbidden to retaliate. However, you and Stephen aren't needed for this mission." With a dismissive wave of his hand, static replaced their images on the screen.

"What have you done!" Somiar stared at him in horror. "Are they okay, did you kill them? I swear if you've hurt either of them..." She lowered her voice, making sure her children didn't hear, "I don't care who the fuck you are, you'll pay."

Her words were a kick in the gut. He was a stranger to his own kids. If Somiar knew anything about him, she would know that no matter what Leila had done, he could never harm her. "I'd never hurt any of you. Stephen and Leila are fine."

Lucien took a step toward him. "You barge in here with the face of a man we all know is dead. Start ranting and performing parlor tricks you claim you learned in your new life." Lucien took another step forward and studied his face. "You trick my niece and nephews into trusting you."

"How dare you!" Somiar's hands curled to fists. "How dare you use my children to manipulate us."

"Rich." Jude leaned in close so the others couldn't hear. "You need to get on with it. It's getting hard to hold everyone's emotions in check. Especially your kids."

Richard gave a slight nod. Taking a pause to deep breathe, he turned his attention to his daughter. "That wasn't my intention. I've checked on you all from time to time since my grandchildren were born. I found out, too late, that the very young and innocent can see us." He smiled. "I tried to teach them 'grandpa' but it always came out Bubba, so I left it at that."

When he got no response, he continued. "Cyrus isn't who you think he is. In your world, Cyrus was a normal man who betrayed the wrong woman. She loved him, and wanted a life with him. When he found out she was pregnant, he left her. Told her he didn't want to have anything to do with her and if she knew what was good for her, she'd get rid of the brat and pretend they'd never met. She killed him and he ended up in the world I live in now. A world called Haven."

Lucien frowned. "I don't get it. What does any of this have to do with us?"

"His daughter ended up there too. They made me her counselor, because she exhibited some bizarre powers."

Lucien's unsympathetic expression didn't waver. "More bizarre than that shit you did with mom and Stephen?"

Before he could answer, Lucien held up a hand and scoffed. "Don't bother. It doesn't sound like our problem."

Richard turned to whisper to Jude. "You sure you're not draining too much emotion? They're almost robotic."

Jude spoke through clenched teeth. "Believe me, you don't want me to let any of them loose, even a little, right now."

Richard turned his attention back to Lucien. "Unfortunately, she is your problem. Everyone has one or more powers in Haven. When a person has more than three, she or he is a descendant of the Oracles, the original inhabitants."

He clasped his hands in front of him and contemplated each of them in turn. This woman wasn't a descendant. "She's a Dreamer. When she arrived at Haven, she kept her Dreamer powers and got one more. Morphing. She can change her appearance, including gender. Haven has two sacred rules, harm no human, kill no Lespri. Breaking one or both of those rules is punishable by death."

Lucien drew his brows together. "Lespri?"

"The people of Haven. She killed Cyrus when she found him there." His attention moved to Astrid. "She broke the second rule when she attacked you, using her father's appearance."

"What?" Astrid's eyes widened. "Why would a Dreamer attack me? We would never attack one of our own unless it was sanctioned by the Legacy."

Lucien sucked in a breath. "Let me get this straight. She killed her father, pretended to be him, then attacked a woman she's never met? That's the strangest shit I've ever heard." He stroked his goatee. "I hate to repeat myself, but what does that have to do with us?"

"They asked me to be her counselor, even though I killed her mother."

Lucien's eyes widened in disbelief. "Why would they do some fucked-up shit like that!" His gaze darted to the children, who didn't seem to notice his outburst.

"It's okay." Richard was about to place a reassuring hand on his son's arm, then thought better of it. "They can't hear this conversation. We've muted our voices to them."

Somiar made a move toward him, but Malachi held her back. "Don't worry, my love." His voice was calm, almost soothing. "If he has done anything to hurt them. I'll kill him myself."

His declaration seemed to be enough for her. Her shoulders relaxed, but her glare stayed glued to Richard.

Lucien glanced from Somiar back to Richard. "They made you council the woman whose mother you murdered? That's some cold shit. What did you do? Tell her everything's going to be okay? I know I killed your mom and all, but we can look past that." Lucien scoffed. "Hope I never go to Haven."

"That's my deepest wish too, son," Richard said. "Going to Haven would mean you died young."

Astrid ran a hand through her hair. "Okay, you killed her mom. It's fucked up, but it kind of answers the question about why she's after your kids. Sounds like a revenge thing. Why's she pissed at me? I've never met any of them until a few days ago."

"You know her."

Astrid blinked several times and arched a brow. "Come again?"

"The Dreamer is Dannen."

CHAPTER 9

Astrid gasped and clutched onto Lucien to keep her balance.

His embrace tightened. This had to be some kind of a sick joke. "Dannen is dead."

Richard offered her a sympathetic smile. "Well, yes and no. Haven is a community of immortals. A place where the deceased go, if they have a certain gene, and die after age twenty-five, but before their fifty-first birthday. A person doesn't know they have the gene until they end up at Haven. The living knows nothing of its existence. Apparently, I have the gene, and since I was forty-nine when I died, 'poof' here I am."

Lucien kept his arms around Astrid. "Poof? That's your explanation? Poof?"

The curly haired woman with the group spoke up. "I think we may have to start from the beginning." Her speech had a slight southern drawl. "Somiar, who am I?"

Somiar stared at the woman for a moment. "It can't be." She shook her head. "Kalyste? Is it really you?"

When Kalyste nodded, Somiar sniffed and wiped a stray tear from her cheek. "I've been trying to convince myself since your introduction that it couldn't be you. You died years ago. I spent the night at the Lunar hotel to attend your wedding. We were told the next morning that you were killed by a hit and run driver the night before."

Kalyste chuckled. "Yeah. That's a long story." She snuggled up against the muscular dreaded man next to her. "Jude is my husband."

Somiar blinked several times, trying to keep back the tears that were threatening. "I'm so happy for you."

Kalyste's lips stretched to a thin line. "My being here is not a good thing. It's an indication of just how much danger you all are in."

Astrid was finding everything hard to follow. "So let me get this straight. Everyone in this room is connected in some way. The um...undead immortals are here to help us catch a Dreamer undead immortal, who wants to kill all of us."

"Exactly." Kalyste's lips twisted in a wry smile. "Blows your mind, doesn't it?"

Somiar interjected. "So, the people in your world must deal with this shit all the time. I'm sure lots of undead want to settle a score. Why is this different?"

Kalyste crossed the room to a chair. Her husband posted up behind her. "Sit back folks, and hold onto your drawers. I'm about to take you on a wild ride."

CHAPTER 10

Kalyste leaned back in her chair, trying to gauge just how much she should tell them. Of all the fucked-up shit she'd seen the Oracles do over the years, this was the first time humans had to be involved.

"There are some things about Haven I'm not allowed to share. But I can tell you this. Oracles never interfere in a case where a Lespri goes rogue.

"Rouge?" Astrid drew her brows together. "What the hell is that?"

"It's what a Lespri becomes if they break even one of our sacred rules. Harm no human. Kill no immortal. It's the duty of their counselors to become a Lespri soldier in order to hunt them down and deliver the final death."

"That would be me," Richard interjected. "The only way to kill an immortal, is to decapitate them. That's how Dannen killed Cyrus, and it's how she'll die."

Astrid gulped. "That sounds forgiving."

Kalyste cast her a wry smile. "As I said, Oracles never get involved. We are the most powerful of the Lespri, so we have boundaries to keep us from becoming total assholes. You know what they say about absolute power. A rogue must be considered an epic threat for us to intervene."

"Us?" Astrid gave her a sidelong glance. "Are you trying to tell me you all are the all-powerful Oracles?"

"No. Just me." Kalyste glanced at each member of the small group and continued. "I was chosen to help Richard, and Jude's powers were needed to help with you all."

Lucien cast her a suspicious stare. "What's that supposed to mean?"

"Don't you wonder who knocked you out? Or why none of you are freaking out at the sight of us?"

They all exchanged looks.

"Jude's an empath," Kalyste continued. "He can read emotions, and drain them. Whatever emotion you have, he can drain it to an acceptable level. Panic, anger, rage, can be brought to heel. If he drains enough, to where you feel nothing, you pass out."

"Listen, Kalyste," Somiar chimed in. "I know we used to be cool and all, but I don't appreciate anyone fucking around with my psyche like that."

"I understand. I didn't like it either when Jude did it to me, and believe me, we wouldn't have done it if it weren't necessary." Her voice hardened. "But your asses are on the line. All of you, along with Astrid."

"Me?" Astrid licked her lips. "I don't understand. We were best friends. And as far as I know, she doesn't even know him," she said, gesturing at Lucien, "or his sister."

"You were right. She wants them dead because of what Richard did to her mother. He killed her mother, she kills his kids. And don't think she'll stop with them." Kalyste cast a pointed look at the children.

"If she even tries, I'll rip out her liver and feed it to her." Somiar glared at Kalyste.

Malachi embraced his wife. "I know Kalyste said they can't hear us but can we not talk about organ harvesting in front of the children?"

"Kalyste, can you restore their normal hearing?" Somiar asked.

"Sure." Kalyste nodded.

Somiar gathered the triplets to her. "Okay, guys we need you to go to your room while we talk to Bubba and his friends."

"Okay." Julien kissed his mother on the cheek. "Play nice."

Her children hugged her and retreated to their bedroom.

Once the door closed, Astrid turned back to the group of immortals. "I don't mean to sound callous, but what does her beef with you and this family have to do with me?" She leaned against the wall. "I loved her."

Richard folded his arms in front of him. "I spent a lot of time with her in counseling sessions, and her problems didn't start with having to deal with her death. She never dealt with her life. She never forgave you for having it better than she did with the Legacy."

"What?" Astrid gasped.

"Your mother was a Legacy member. Her mother was mediocre, at best. You outshined everyone with your assignments. Never missed a mark. You had it made. Whatever you wanted was yours for the taking, even a place with the Legacy, and you threw it back in their faces."

Richard sighed. "She felt you cheated her of the chance to prove she was better than you. Betrayed all the Dreamers when you left the life, turned your back on who you are."

Astrid rubbed her temples and nibbled on her lip. "But that's not what I did. I didn't know she was so envious of me. I'm not proud of my life as a Dreamer. They made being an assassin sound like a noble profession."

She stared down at her feet and took a deep breath. "I remember the face of every mark I hit. We weren't meant to be enemies with the Catchers, and we damned sure weren't born to be killers."

"She bought into the lies the Legacy told. Their side of the story is we want to keep the Dreamers under our thumb to diminish their numbers," Richard explained. "She has it in her head that after she finishes all of you off, phase two of her plan can be started."

"And just what is phase two?" Lucien asked.

"Capturing Catchers and using them as breeders to create more Dreamers." Richard shook his head. "None of us knew until you were born that Dreamers can have more than one child if they mate with a Catcher. It had never been done after we became enemies. Dreamers can only have one child. And they're always girls. Unless their mate is a Catcher."

"But that doesn't make sense." Astrid frowned. "Some of the children will be boys."

Richard scoffed. "And they will either be killed or enslaved until they are of breeding age."

Astrid ran a hand through her hair. "She's gone slap crazy. There's no way she'll be able to hide an entire enslaved race."

"And that's where she thinks Haven will come in," Kalyste said. "She's planning on taking it over. It'll never happen. The Oracles will band together and move Heaven and Earth before they let her have reign. Right now, they're only risking one Oracle. Me."

"I don't see a problem." Lucien paced the small space. "If all the Oracles banding together can stop her, why not do it?"

"Because it will alert too many people of our existence. Do you really think she's going to stay out of public view? She'll make sure we're all exposed. Dozens of supernatural beings laying a whammy on one person isn't going to go unnoticed." Kalyste shook her head.

"They're giving us seven days to handle this. After that, they intervene. Thousands of humans will die as collateral damage, and Haven will no longer be a paradise, it'll be chaos. We will have broken our own laws. Humans and Lespri will lose their lives."

Richard turned to Somiar and Malachi. "You've been awfully quiet."

"What do you want me to say? Hey, dad, nice to see you. Glad you're undead." Somiar rolled her eyes. "Look, it's not you I'm mad at. I'd made my peace with mom about the situation, but seeing you has opened some old wounds. I never got the chance to know you, and knowing I will probably never see you again after this is over makes me want to steer clear of any emotional ties."

Richard tried to hold his composure.

Kalyste felt sorry for him. He turned his back to the group, but he was facing her, and she could see the unshed tears.

"I understand." Richard paused a moment and turned back around. "Kalyste, Jude, and I have a plan. It will involve splitting you up. We don't want Dannen tracking any of you here."

He looked to Lucien. "For the protection of the rest of the Catchers and staff here, we want you and Astrid up top. We can stay at your place. Somiar and Malachi need to stay here with the children."

Malachi stepped forward and scowled. "No way am I going to let them face that psycho alone."

"Yes, you are," Lucien corrected. "Your family needs you. Somiar and I know what it's like to lose a father. Your children don't need that."

"I'm with Lucien." Astrid spoke up. "Dannen was my friend, or so I thought. This is personal."

"Seven days." Kalyste spoke softly. "Lucien and Astrid, I need you to hold my hand. I'll transport us to your house. The clock starts ticking, now."

Chapter 11

Astrid fought the slight wave of dizziness when they appeared in Lucien's living room.

"Don't worry." Kalyste pat her on the shoulder. "People usually feel a little sick the first time they teleport. It shouldn't be a problem next time."

"Wow!" Lucien exclaimed. "Now that's the way to travel." His smile showed he wasn't any the worse for wear.

Astrid couldn't resist smiling back. Those dimples were too damned sexy. "I'll bet you were the kid who always headed straight for the rollercoaster."

"Damned straight. They were the best rides." He glanced around the room, then at Kalyste. "Where are the rest of the big bads?"

Kalyste laughed. "If you're talking about Richard and Jude, they scoured the house, learning every nook and cranny, looking for anything that would make us vulnerable. They're probably back at Haven by now." She stepped to the center of the room. "I'm going to join them, but don't worry, I'll be here in a blink if you need anything."

Astrid was uncertain of what to do now. She was keenly aware they were alone. She could feel Lucien's gaze on her back. She shuffled her feet and looked around the room.

He was clearly a bachelor. Black leather furniture, light gray walls. Clothes scattered on the sofa and over chairs. A pair of worn boxing gloves tossed in the corner. There wasn't a feminine touch anywhere.

"I thought Catchers kept their houses impenetrable." She plucked a pink stuffed rabbit from the corner of the couch and smiled. "Friend of yours?"

He chuckled. "Ruby's. She left him for me in case I get lonely." He took the toy from her and returned it to the couch.

His cheeks rounded in an attractive blush. Had his complexion not been so dark, she would swear he would have turned red.

"We keep our houses well protected against normal people and Dreamers." He rubbed his palms on his jeans as if she hadn't just seen him be protective of a fake rabbit. "But there's nothing normal about what we're dealing with."

Astrid leaned against the chair. "Just when I thought my life was coming together. Got the business I wanted, mostly free of the Legacy, and very little drama."

Lucien lifted a brow. "What do you mean, *mostly* free of the Legacy?"

"Oh, come now. Do you think the Legacy would really let me go, no strings attached? I'm sure they've been watching me. What I haven't figured out is why no one came to find out why I was dumped at your doorstep, half dead. They should have gotten to me before you did."

"You think your little friend got the drop on the Dreamer assigned to you?" Lucien went to the kitchen, came back with two bottles of water, and handed one to Astrid.

"Oh, God." She held the cool bottle to her head. "I hadn't until you said it." Opening the bottle, she took a drink. "I can't believe she's been so troubled all this time. This doesn't sound like the Dannen I grew up with." Astrid fought back tears. To think someone hated her that much. Someone who wasn't a Catcher.

"So, what now?"

Lucien offered his hand. "Now I show you the house. No telling how long you're going to have to hang your hat here."

"Apparently, no more than seven days." She stood up, ignoring his hand. "Lead the way."

***

Lucien had to hand it to Astrid. She was handling things well. Finding out your best friend is not only undead, but wants you dead is a bitter pill to swallow. Through everything, she kept a brave front. He just hoped she stayed this strong.

He showed her around the lower level, then up the spiral staircase, stopping at the third door in the hall. "This is your room." He pointed to the door at the end of the corridor. "That one is mine." He held her door open and stepped aside for her to enter.

"Wow, this is a lot of space." The light-gray walls were adorned with beautiful, bright artwork and scenic photographs. There was a sitting area with plush chairs and a couch. She went to the massive, ornate wardrobe across from the sitting area. Pocket doors concealed a large flat screened television.

Lucien came up beside her and opened a drawer under the tv. "The remotes are in here. Speakers and iPhone station are in the cabinet underneath." He pointed at the cherry wood night stand next to the king-sized bed. "There are phone stations with speakers on both nightstands, so it doesn't matter what side you sleep on."

She smiled weakly. "I don't have a side of the bed. I'm usually all over the place." She crossed the hardwood floor. "Is this the bathroom?"

Before he could answer, she pushed the levered doorknob. There was a large jetted tub, and separate shower. A water closet housed the toilet. Another door next to the linen closet boasted a large walk-in closet, full of women's clothes. She turned back to Lucien. "Whose clothes are these?"

He stood behind her, open-mouthed. "I have no idea where these came from."

Astrid spied an envelope with her name on it resting on the dresser. She pulled out the page inside and read out loud. "I think I got your size right. No problem to change if needed. Underclothes in dresser. Regards, Kalyste."

Lucien laughed. "I guess she thought of everything."

"No kidding." Astrid closed the door and made her way back to the bedroom.

"Any idea how we're going to keep Dannen out of here? I know your house is protected from Dreamers, but how about immortal Dreamers on steroids?"

Lucien stroked the 5 o'clock shadow on his chin. "Kalyste says she's got it covered. There's another Lespri guarding the house. Has the power to form force fields."

Astrid went to sit on the couch in front of the television. "I don't like being used as bait."

"Not my favorite thing either, but this isn't the first time I've had a nutcase trying to kill me."

Astrid rested her head against the back of the sofa. "Well, it's a first for me. I've always been the hunter, not the hunted."

The words jarred Lucien back to just who he was dealing with. "Listen, I don't mean to sound like an asshole or anything, but how many people have you killed?"

She narrowed her eyes and scoffed, "How many have you? How many have Malachi, or Stephen, or Somiar?" She picked up a throw pillow and hugged it to her. "Can we please not do the 'you're worse than I am,' thing?"

She plucked at a thread on the arm of the couch. "It's almost funny," she muttered. "I thought it would be the Legacy who came after me."

Lucien sat next to her, instantly sorry for the question. "I owe you an apology. We've all done things we weren't proud of in the name of our causes."

"And look what it got us." She hung her head.

"Hey." He lifted her chin. "We're going to be okay."

He gazed at her lips, full and inviting. When she didn't pull away, he leaned in close, and brushed her lips with his.

Astrid inhaled, "This might be a bad idea," she murmured, never breaking contact with his lips.

He pulled back slightly. The last thing he needed was a relationship, especially with her. If they were going to do this, there had to be an understanding. "Do you want me to stop?"

***

Her head was telling her yes, but her body said no. *What the hell, we might not see tomorrow.*

Without a word, she cupped the back of his head, deepening the kiss. She maneuvered him back against the cushions and straddled his lap.

When her hands started on his buttons, he captured them in his. "I need to hear the words, Astrid. Do you want this? No strings. No promises."

The sound of her name on his lips made her heart flutter and her panties wet. "I want this, no strings. No promises."

He released her hands, letting her finish working on his buttons. His hands yanked her t-shirt from her jeans, drawing it over her head.

She closed her eyes, immersing herself in the moment. Impatient with his buttons, she ripped his shirt open. The sprinkle of hair on his chest teased her fingers. Muscles rippled under her palms. Leaning forward, she traced his nipples with her tongue, a slight smile curving her lips at his sharp intake.

His arms encircled her, palms on her back, freeing the clasp on her black lacy bra.

Pulling back, she allowed him to gaze at her exposed breasts and raised herself slightly to undo his jeans, while he undid hers.

He slid his arms under her buttocks and stood, her legs around his waist.

She deepened her kiss, her tongue sliding against his, her hands wanting to be everywhere at once.

He carried her to the bed, and gently settled her on her back. He kissed down her chest pausing to caress each nipple with his lips and tongue while one hand traced the skin above the waistband of her pants. Kissing his way down her abdomen, he paused at her navel tasting the sensitive skin around it.

Pulling her pants off, he inhaled. "You smell so good, Astrid. I wonder if you taste as good as you smell."

Her pussy tingled in anticipation. "Go ahead and find out, baby."

Without another word, the tip of his wet, warm tongue lightly slid across her clit, almost making her explode right then and there.

Good gracious, this man knew what he was doing. It'd been too long since she'd gotten a god lay.

Not wanting to grab his head and hump against him like a maniac, she grasped at the comforter, bunching in her fists.

He pressed against her, applying more pressure to her pussy with his tongue. Sliding licking, sucking at her as if she were the most delectable flavor of ice cream. And she was melting. Fast.

Scooting away from him, she denied herself the pleasure of release. She got on all fours and leaned forward teasing his lips with hers. Her taste and scent lingered on him exciting her own senses.

She sat back on her feet and leveled a teasing smile his way. "My turn. Lie back."

After he complied, she yanked his pants down past his muscular thighs then calves and dropped them to the floor.

Hot damn! Black boxer briefs. Sexy as hell. She loved a man who cared as much about his drawers as he did his outerwear.

She ran a finger along the waistband, running her tongue along her bottom lip. When he lifted his hips off the bed, she slid them down, tossing them to the floor to join his pants.

Starting at his ankles, she kissed and tongued a path to his groin, stopping to suck on his throbbing dick. She wrapped her fingers around the thick base, taking care not to gag herself. He definitely tasted as good as he smelled. Delicious.

Lucien ran his hands through her hair, pressing her down on him. She licked and sucked until strong hands gripped her under her arms. "No, baby. I don't want to be done with you yet."

Hmmm. A giver. Intrigued, she rose until she hovered over him, face to face. Never letting her gaze leave his, she lowered herself onto him, sighing at the sensation of her pussy being filled.

His lids lowered, his hands on her ass, guiding himself deeper.

Shit. This was going to take some patience. She sat straight up, her palms on his chest, controlling the pace and depth of their lovemaking. She stroked him, slow and steady. "No need to rush, my Lucien."

She moved her hips in slow circles while sliding up and down his rock-hard dick, gauging his response, wanting him to be as excited as she.

His eyes were closed, but she caught glimpses of the whites as they rolled back. Her desire growing, she increased her pace.

Knowing she was on the edge of release, she slowed, wanting to match his, but he wasn't having it. He wrapped his arms around her back. Pulling her close against him. Once in his tight embrace her slid one hand to her buttocks holding her immobile as he took control of the pace. The animal part of her surrendered. She let herself go, soaking his dick with her release, along with his groan of completion.

Rolling onto her back, she took a deep breath. "Wow."

He rose to his side propping himself up on an elbow. "Any regrets?"

Astrid nibbled at the corner of her lower lip, then smiled. "Not one. My body needed this. I've been way too stressed out."

Lucien chuckled. "Wow, I'm a human stress ball."

"A cute one. At least I didn't squeeze your head, expecting your eyes to bulge out."

They both burst into laughter.

Astrid stretched. "So, I think I'm gonna hit the shower, then settle in for the night. You're welcome to join me."

Lucien ran a finger across her abdomen in an absent caress. "No, I'll go to my room and do the same." He rose from the bed and stepped into his pants. Before turning to leave, he kissed her forehead. "I'll see you in the morning."

Astrid smiled. "See you in the morning."

As she watched his retreating back, she silently kicked herself. *Damn, it would have been so much better if I hadn't invited him to stay and kissed him off.*

Chapter 12

L ucien sat at the kitchen table, caressing a cup of coffee. Always an early riser, he enjoyed the solitude.

After leaving Astrid last night he had to take a cool shower. When she invited him to stay with her, the last thing he wanted to do was leave. He wanted to spend the night making love to her, but considering the danger they had to face, he decided they both needed rest.

Damn! What kind of fool was he? He got no sleep. At least with her, he would have enjoyed being awake.

"Mind if I join you, son?" Richard appeared at the opposite end of the table and without waiting for Lucien to answer, pulled out a chair to sit.

"How do you do that?" Lucien placed his mug on the table and sat back in his chair, arms folded. "You just pop in here like it's the most natural thing in the world."

Richard raised a brow. "You seem to be handling it pretty well."

"Would hysterics make you feel better? What am I supposed to do?" Lucien watched his father's face, looking for something, anything that gave him a clue as to what he was thinking.

Nothing.

After a brief pause, Richard looked away first. "I never intended to show up at all. I'm dead to you and I had planned to stay that way."

"Yeah, yeah, yeah. But some crazy girl whose mother you iced is now after me and anyone else connected to you." Lucien scraped his chair back and poured another mug of coffee.

"What kind of sadistic assholes run that place, anyway? Did they really think she would be okay with you giving her advice? Seems like things are more fucked up there than they are here."

When Richard didn't respond, Lucien stroked his chin. The only man in his life he'd truly grieved, the man he'd begged God to let him spend more time with, sat across from him.

What do you do when a wish is granted? Grateful wasn't what came to mind.

A sicko was after him and he had to work with a Dreamer he didn't fully trust. Not to mention the sicko wanted not only him, but his whole family dead. It was like being granted a wish from a genie. You can have it, but it's going to cost you.

Lucien contemplated his father over the rim of his coffee mug. "I've been getting to know mom."

That struck a nerve. A glimmer of malice reached his father's eyes.

"Yes, I know. I also know she's with Stephen now. Didn't think my old partner had it in him to love a Dreamer."

"Neither did you. Granted, you didn't know she was a Dreamer when you fell in love and married her." Lucien carefully placed his cup on the table. "Had you known, would you have still loved her?"

"We'll never know, will we?" Richard's lips curled into a sneer as he rose from his chair and set to pacing.

Lucien cocked his head crossed his arms. "Did you ever get a vision of her?"

Richard briefly paused his steps to contemplate his son. "What are you talking about?"

"Ah, yes." Lucien sat back in his chair and stretched his legs. "You died before we found out about the visions. I'm sure you know some history of the Dreamers and Catchers' connection?"

At Richard's nod, Lucien continued. "We didn't put everything we found through an ancestor's diary out there. The part about a Catcher's vision is a little known fact. If a Catcher is with a Dreamer, and she is his true mate, he will see her in visions. It happened to Malachi when he got with Somiar." He sat forward, elbow on the table, his chin resting in his hand. "Did you ever see mom?"

"No."

Lucien tried not to let his disappointment show. He hadn't realized until that moment how much he wanted his parents' tale to be one of an epic love.

"I may not have gotten this vision you talk about, but I did love her. That being said, I don't think I can ever forgive her for hiding my daughter from me. Or for deserting us. She should have trusted me with the truth." Raising a dismissive hand, he exhaled loudly. "But that's ancient history and I have no desire to keep hashing it out. I've done enough of that over the years. The Oracles knew I would be distracted by her, which is why they're keeping her out of it."

Lucien stood and leaned forward, his hands resting on the table. He cleared his throat in a subtle attempt to force his father to meet his gaze. "What do you mean by that? Don't you remember the woman you married?"

When Richard didn't cease in his mission to wear a hole in the kitchen floor, Lucien continued. "Do you really think she's going to sit around and let this happen without her? I'm surprised she and

Stephen aren't at the Catcher station or trying to beat the door down here."

Richard stopped his pacing and pinned Lucien with a flinty stare. "The Catchers aren't the only ones who can erase memories. Neither she nor Stephen remember what's going on. Dannen knows there's no love lost between Leila, Stephen, and I, so she's not after them."

"Wow," Lucien scoffed. "So, if we don't live, they won't know the truth. That's some cold shit."

Richard's scowl darkened. "We do what we have to do to survive."

"If we succeed, are you going to erase all of our memories too?"

"No. Who's going to believe you if you spill the beans about us?" His words sounded as casual as a man discussing the weather.

"Gee, thanks, dad." Lucien's voice dripped with sarcasm. "You're swell." He reclaimed his seat at the table and drummed his fingers on top.

He didn't know the man his father had become. The loving man he'd known when he was a kid was gone. Keeping him at arm's length would probably be the best thing to do. Had to treat him like a stranger. That's the only way he would be able to work with him, and keep his sanity.

"So why don't you tell me our next move?"

"I'd like to know that as well." Astrid strode into the room. "Coffee cups?" She addressed Lucien, her expression neutral.

"Middle cabinet," he answered with a tilt of his head. Lucien studied her as she made her way around the kitchen, pouring a cup of coffee and rummaging through the fridge, retrieving the ingredients for a cheese omelet.

"Have you two eaten?"

"I could eat," Lucien replied. "Just had coffee this morning. Never learned to cook. I didn't even know that stuff was in the fridge."

Richard chuckled. "You can thank Kalyste later. She supplied the food."

Astrid cracked eggs into a bowl and turned to Richard. "Do you eat?"

"If you're asking if I get hungry, the answer is no. My people eat purely for pleasure."

"Must be nice," Astrid mumbled. "I'll make you a plate."

"Thanks, but I'm not staying. I'm going to join the others at Haven, but we're keeping you under our protection. If Dannen comes anywhere near the place, we'll be here before you can blink." Before either of them could answer, Richard disappeared.

Lucien continued to study Astrid, looking for any sign that she regretted their tryst.

She reached for a pan on a shelf over the counter, her shirt riding up, exposing the smooth brown flesh on her stomach. He remembered the way her skin tasted on his tongue. Only a couple of inches higher were the breasts he'd feasted on the night before. He was grateful to be seated. No doubt his dick would advertise what he was thinking had he been standing.

***

Astrid continued her task, hoping she gave nothing away as she cooked. She wasn't really hungry, but she needed something to keep her busy while she was in the room with Lucien.

She didn't regret fucking him last night, but she did regret asking him to spend the night with her. When he turned her down, she wasn't sure what to think. Rejection from a man wasn't something she was used to.

It irritated her that he didn't seem bothered at all this morning. Like last night never happened. She plated the omelets for the two of them and took a seat.

Everything was tasteless to her, but he attacked his food as if it was the last time he'd enjoy a meal.

She dropped her fork to her plate with a clatter, and arched a brow when he met her gaze. "If we're going to continue working together, we need to stop pretending last night didn't happen and set some ground rules."

"Shit." Lucien sighed and set his fork aside. "I didn't take you for the 'what did our night together mean' type."

Her eyes widened and she twisted her lips in a smirk. "Are you shitting me right now? I'm not interested in exploring what last night meant. It was, what it was."

"Then why are you so bothered?" He ran a finger under his lower lip with a smug look that made her want to slap the donkey shit out of him.

"I thought maybe I played myself by asking you to stay. Believe it or not lover-man, the request was because I like your dick. And I wasn't tired." She sat back in her chair, her gaze never leaving his. "I have no interest in a relationship."

Lucien sat back in his chair, the shit-eating grin faltering for a second before it was plastered back on his lips. "Hm. For a minute there, you deflated my balloon."

"Don't worry about it. Like I said, I like your dick. I'm sure I could get it re-inflated."

He laughed. "So, we're good?"

Astrid chuckled. "Yeah. We're good." Relieved they'd gotten the morning after awkwardness out of the way, she scooped her eggs on her fork and savored her breakfast. "You get the feeling your dad knows what happened?"

"Pretty sure he does. They're keeping an eye on us, but I don't think they watched us fuck. Be a pretty pervy thing to do."

She finished the last of her meal. "So, what do we do now?"

"Wait for the big bad wolf to strike like the fatted lambs we are."

Astrid barely had time for the words to register before Jude appeared next to her. "What are you doing here? Where's Kalyste?"

Jude smiled, but it didn't reach his eyes. "Sleep, Astrid."

The last thing she remembered before the world went black was Dannen ramming her blade into Lucien's chest.

CHAPTER 13

Astrid scanned the living room, realizing she was in her Dreamer body. What the hell happened? Why did Kalyste's husband knock her out?

She remembered seeing Dannen stab Lucien, and ran at top speed to the kitchen.

Before she could cross the threshold, Dannen stepped in front of her and punched her in the throat. She quickly healed herself, but didn't have time to stand before Dannen straddled her chest, a rueful smile on her lips.

Instead of finishing her off, Dannen stood and offered a hand. "You're going to have to learn to control your impulsiveness." Dannen's face contorted and changed until it was replaced by Kalyste.

"Now there's an oxymoron if I've ever heard one." Astrid hopped to her feet unassisted and took a step back, not sure who or what she was talking to. "What the hell was that!"

"Sorry to take you by surprise like that, but Dannen isn't going to warn you she's coming." Kalyste went to stand next to Lucien, who for a dead man, looked surprisingly...alive.

Lucien stalked away from Kalyste and leaned against the table. "I don't care what the lesson was supposed to be, I don't appreciate being mock stabbed and knocked out."

"You'd appreciate it even less if I'd really been Dannen and stabbed you," Kalyste shot back.

"I had to do that to you." Jude appeared next to Kalyste and put an arm around her waist. "We thought you needed to be ready for when I really have to knock you out at a moment's notice."

Astrid had gotten so used to people popping in and out of the room, Jude's sudden appearance didn't faze her. "Why would you have to knock us out at a moment's notice?"

"Not him." Jude jerked a thumb at Lucien. "You." He pinned her with his gaze. "The only reason I knocked Lucien out this time was because I didn't want him to give away that this was a trick. In an actual situation, I'd knock you out because you'll need your Dreamer body to fight, and instant sleep on demand isn't a thing for humans."

Astrid inhaled sharply. "Wait a minute. Why am I able to project here? Since this is a Catcher's house, the stones should keep me from using my Dreamer body."

Kalyste nibbled on her bottom lip. "We had to disable them."

Lucien inhaled sharply. His body stiffened and his jaw clenched. "You did what! The Catcher stones are the only things keeping every Dreamer out for my blood from invading my home. Why don't you just serve me up on a platter to the Legacy?"

"Astrid's going to need her Dreamer powers to fight Dannen. We still have the house protected against other Dreamers and Lespri." Kalyste held up a hand before Lucien could interrupt. "Nikolai is an immortal who can generate force fields. He has one covering the house. But we're going to have to let it down to give Dannen a chance to get at you two."

Astrid frowned. How could the Lespri be so dense? She rubbed her temples, and took a breath. She wanted to carefully select her words, not wanting to offend Kalyste. After all the Lepri were needed if any of them were going to get through this alive. "Dannen may be a loose cannon, but she's not stupid. She's going to know it's a trap when the force field suddenly comes down."

Kalyste smiled. "We've got it covered. Someone she's trusted into her circle has the job of making it look like she's taken care of Nikolai."

"I'm surprised she trusts any of you people." Astrid said.

"The woman she's befriended doesn't like me," Kalyste grimaced. "In fact, she hates me, so Dannen thought she was the easiest one to bring to her side."

Astrid scoffed. "Then why in hell do you trust her?"

"She may hate me, but she loves Haven. And she knows the Oracles will destroy her if they have to get involved. There's no way she's going to betray them."

"Well, isn't that just perfect?" Lucien threw his arms up in exasperation. "Where's my dad?"

"You won't be seeing him again until the final fight. He has to be the one to take Dannen's head." Kalyste's voice was soft. Almost mournful. "That's the way he wanted it."

***

Lucien stared at Kalyste, not sure he'd heard her right. His father had missed out on years of his life, and all of his daughter's. Even though he'd checked on them from time to time, was he really going to rob Somiar of the chance to get to know him? Had he become so entrenched in his new life that they'd been reduced to just the means he would use to catch his mark?

Anger like he'd never felt bubbled in his chest until it exploded from his lips. "What the fuck do you mean, that's the way he wants it?"

"Watch your tone with my wife, man." Jude's slight Jamaican accent became more pronounced as he stepped in front of Kalyste.

Astrid put a gentle hand on Lucien's shoulder and stroked his back. "Take it easy. Let's hear what they have to say."

Concentrating on the feel of Astrid's hand rhythmically stroking his back, Lucien mentally counted to ten. It wasn't their fault his father was being an asshole. A sense of calm enveloped him. He didn't know if it was Astrid's touch soothing him, or Jude draining some of his emotions.

"It's not me," Jude said with a barely perceptible smile.

Lucien tried to hide the shock from his face and repeated his question in a less confrontational manner. "Why doesn't my father want to see me?"

"Because you can't have more. He can never be part of your, nor your sister's life in any real way again. You two are grown, making your own decisions. Had it not been for Dannen, you would have never known of his existence."

If it hadn't been for Astrid at his side, her calming hand on his back, Lucien wasn't sure he would have been able to contain his anger. He clenched his fist until his fingers cramped.

The more he learned about these fucked up people, the more he disliked them. He was perfectly fine when he thought his father was dead and buried. Now he had to live with the fact that he was around, and didn't want to see him until it served his purpose. He'd had enough to deal with in his life. People he'd never met wanted him dead. First the Legacy, now this psycho bitch from hell.

"Your father will be with you for the final battle. He'll fight beside you, and we'll make sure you have everything you need." Kalyste's lips quivered when she spoke. There was something in her gaze that told him she wanted to say more. He caught the shake of Jude's head when she looked at him..

Without another word, Jude and Kalyste disappeared.

***

Astrid put a hand on Lucien's chest. "I'm sorry." Knowing how lame her words were, she tried to think of something else to say. Something that would make him feel better.

Lucien refused to meet her gaze. Gathering the plates from the table, he carefully placed them in the sink as if the task was the most important thing in the world.

She noted the remnants on the plates had become hard and en-crusted. "How long were we out? That food seems to have been there a while."

He held a dish under hot water until the particles loosened. "A couple of hours. They couldn't agree on whether or not ambushing us was a god idea." He never stopped to look at her.

Plate under the water, in the dishwasher, cup under the water, in the dishwasher, repeat. When all the dishes were loaded, he leaned over the sink, bracing his elbows on the edge. "He doesn't love us."

Astrid stood planted in place as if her feet had taken root. Raised as a Dreamer, displays of affection from a parent weren't a thing. She'd always assumed her mother loved her because that's what mothers did.

Not once had she heard I love you from her mother, but the lack of words didn't hurt her feelings. Dreamers knew that the death of their mother was part of the risk of the job. If it happened, you got pissed, got even, then moved on. It never occurred to her that Catchers weren't brought up the same way.

Unsure of what would make him feel better, she came up behind him and wrapped her arms around his waist, pressing her body against his back.

He turned in her embrace, and looked down at her.

His expression held a question, but she wasn't sure what it was. His gaze lowered, to her lips. She instinctively licked them, her lids fluttering closed, preparing for the kiss she was sure to come. When nothing happened, she opened her eyes.

The look in his eyes was eerie. He stared at her as if it were the first time he'd seen her. He backed away, his flinty gaze never breaking from hers. "We have to prepare for the rest of the day." He turned and briskly strode away, never looking back.

***

Lucien sat behind the desk in his study and rested his forehead in his hands. He tried to make sense of what he'd just seen and felt just before he was about to kiss Astrid. In that brief moment the room fell away and he was in a cemetery standing before a closed coffin. A tear escaped and he was enveloped in sorrow. In a blink, he was back in his kitchen standing in front of Astrid, her eyes closed, waiting for his kiss.

What the hell? It couldn't have been a vision. Was his soulmate dead? Who the hell was in the coffin? He sat back and contemplated the ceiling wating for answers to come.

CHAPTER 14

Astrid reclined on the several pillows stacked on her bed and stared at the ceiling. In her mind she replayed the scene in the kitchen, trying to find the exact moment she'd done whatever it was that made him close himself off to her.

Consoling others in their time of sorrow wasn't her strong suit. Dreamers weren't raised to wallow in grief, even for a short time. When her mother was killed, she was sad, but the Legacy immediately took over her training. She hadn't been given time to grieve.

Same scenario with Dannen's mom. Dannen was horrified about what had happened but years of conditioning by the Legacy kept her from dwelling on it. She was killed in the line of duty. Simple as that.

The hairs on the back of her neck stood on end and her spine tingled. She tried to push the sensation aside. Usually, it meant there was another Dreamer close by.

The fact that she wasn't in her Dreamer body gave her pause. She exhaled slow and steady.

Had to be a case of nerves. Murdered best friend trying to kill her, the undead popping in and out, staying in the house of a man who was suddenly acting like she had leprosy.

Her life had become a heaping, steamy platter of crap.

Since she had been assured the house was shielded by the Lespri, she tried not to worry, but instinct wouldn't let it be.

Sliding from the bed to the floor, she inched across the carpet, staying low, and crouched in the corner. Resting her back against the wall, she bent her knees until her heels grazed her butt and rested her forehead on her knees. She wrapped her arms around her legs and closed her eyes, letting her other senses take over.

The air stirred with an uninvited energy. Inhaling, she found a place of calm in her core, and evened her breathing.

Relief flooded her when she opened her eyes to find herself in her closet. She ran her hand over her short hair, and fingered the sword and daggers always strapped to her Dreamer body when on assignment. The foreboding sense that she wasn't alone increased. She peered out the door to the bathroom and stealthily made her way to the bedroom. Her Dreamer body would do her no good if someone killed her sleeping body.

The bedroom was empty, but the air still crackled with an evil energy.

Where the hell were the Lespri? They had to feel this almost de-monic force.

A faint glow shimmered in the center of the room. Her double emerged from the light, sword drawn, an evil smirk distorting her features.

"What the fuck!" Before she could recover from her shock, her look-alike swung her arm in a graceful arc and sliced a deep gash in Astrid's arm.

The wound healed instantly. It normally took her a few seconds to heal. The Legacy were the only Dreamers with instantaneous healing ability.

Not taking anymore time to ponder her new-found gift, she grabbed her sword from behind her right shoulder, and pulled it from the sheath strapped to her back. She tapped the quick release button at her chest and the sheath fell from her body, leaving her able to move more freely.

"I know it's you, Dannen. I'm sorry it's come to this." She circled her enemy, their gazes locked. "I loved you like a sister. What have I done to make you hate me so much?"

Without a word, Dannen rushed toward her, fury marring the face that matched hers. Her sword raised high in one hand, a long gold handled dagger poised in the other.

Astrid leaned, back, low enough for Dannen's dagger to stab the air above her, then rolled on the carpet. She grabbed Dannen's legs, letting her own weight and the weight of the sword send her crashing onto a wooden table, shattering it as if it were made of toothpicks.

She jumped to her feet, looking down at Dannen. "What happened? What did I do to make you hate me so much?"

"You know exactly what you did, you condescending bitch," Dannen spat. "I saw the pity in your face every time you looked at me."

Dannen disappeared from the floor and emerged across the room, twirling her sword in her hand. "*You* had the mother who was a Legacy member. *You* had the prestige, treated like the sun rose from your ass because *you* were next in line." She clenched her teeth, jaw muscles twitching. "You thought you were so much better than me."

This bitch has gone absolutely crazy. All the time they'd spent together growing up, the shared secrets, helping each other practice.

Even giving the other the time to mourn their mothers when the Legacy wouldn't.

"I've always loved you, Dannen. I've never thought I was better than you. Deep down, you know that. I think the problem we have here, is *you* think I'm better than you."

Dannen dropped her weapons. She screamed and charged at Astrid, fingers curled to fists.

***

Lucien reached Astrid's room at the same time Richard popped in.

Shit, he wished he could zap himself wherever he wanted to go.

The scene unfolding in front of him was like something from a sci-fi movie. If he were the kind to take drugs, he would have sworn he was on a bad acid trip. Frozen to the spot, he watched in confusion as Astrid fought...herself.

Elbowing Richard, Lucien yelled. "What the hell! I thought the place was protected."

"One of them is Dannen." Richard pressed his back against the wall outside the room and closed his eyes. "I'm trying to get a read on which one, but there's too much movement."

Lucien marveled at the scene in front of him. What he was witnessing was personal. The women were beating the shit out each other with their bare hands. One was getting it a lot worse than the other. He prayed Astrid was the better fighter, but he couldn't be sure.

Kalyste appeared against the wall next to Richard. "About time you showed up. I've enhanced Astrid's Dreamer power to heal, but we need to put a stop to this and take Dannen down."

Lucien gasped. "Enhance her powers? You can do that?"

"Yes." Kalyste took a quick glance in the room. "I'm an *akitvateur*. I can enhance a power, even turn it against its owner." She bit her lip. "I was able to enhance Astrid's healing power before the fight, but now they're so mixed up, I can't tell them apart."

Lucien winced as one of the women was hurled across the room, connecting face first against the wall, the force of her body cracking the plaster. "So, who's who?" He gazed at the women, trying to find a clue.

The woman hauled herself form the floor. Blood caking her face and hair. Within a few seconds, she was healed.

Lucien clutched Richard's arm. "That one is Dannen. If Kalyste enhanced Astrid's powers, Dannen can't heal as fast."

Richard's clothes instantly changed to a red and black form fitting armor. He sprinted into the room, sword raised and connected the blade to his foe's neck. The blade didn't slice through, but Dannen couldn't hold on to her form as Astrid.

Holding her throat, blood spewing between her fingers, Dannen lunged behind Astrid, grabbing her around the waist. They disappeared.

CHAPTER 15

Astrid jerked out of Dannen's grasp. Ready for their fight to continue, she fingered the handles of the daggers strapped to each thigh. Damn. Her sword was still back at the house.

At least Dannen no longer looked like her. She took in the stone walls surrounding them. Damp earth beneath their feet. The dank air was warm and humid, causing small beads of sweat on her forehead. Silver lanterns lit with candles hung from the stone ceiling. "Where the hell are we, you crazy bitch?"

Dannen, still clutching her bloody throat, sneered at Astrid, and settled on a large boulder. A few seconds later, the wound was fully healed. "That asshole almost took me out." A humorless chuckle erupted from her lips. "Being dead has it's rewards."

Astrid withdrew her daggers. "I asked you a question." She spoke between clenched teeth, taking care to keep her temper in check. Making Dannen lose hers was the goal. Dannen always got fifty kinds of careless when she lost it.

Dannen continued to study her while toying with a lock of her matted hair. You're in no position to to ask questions."

"Oh, I think I am." Astrid twirled her daggers. "You can't beat me, Dannen. You never could." She re-sheathed her knives. "How did it feel living in my shadow? Always wanting to be me? Wanting the life I had, the mother I had, the friends. I don't know why I ever bothered with you. You're nothing but a loser."

Dannen's lips curled in a smile that didn't reach her eyes. "All that is about to change." She turned and faced the back of the cave, shrouded in darkness. "Ladies," she yelled.

Five young women, of all shapes and sizes emerged from the shadow, rolling a large cage alongside them. Inside were three middle aged women Astrid didn't recognize. The women retreated back into the darkness.

"What's going on?" Astrid's eybrows drew together in a frown. "Who are they?"

"You mean I know something you don't?" A maniacal laugh rang throughout the cave. Dannen placed her finger to her lower lip and tilted her head. "Oh, that's right." Her voice dripped with sarcasm. "You've never met them in the flesh. So to speak."

Dannen walked over and rattled the bars of the cage.

The imprisoned women never spoke, never moved. They gazed with stony expressions at Dannen, casting a fleeting glance at Astrid.

"Astrid, meet the Legacy."

Astrid gasped. "It can't be. I don't believe you. They would never let you near them." She looked between Dannen and the Legacy. "How do you know who they are? You don't have the fighting talent to beat them."

"I may not have the talent if they were in their Dreamer bodies. This is them, in the flesh." Dannen rubbed her hands together. "As I said, being dead has its advantages. Some of the Lespri were smart enough to follow me. One has the handy little talent for sniffing out other powers. Another is a teleporter. She was able to take them before they knew what was happening."

"You can't do this." Astrid licked suddenly dry lips. "You'll have the rest of the Legacy, and the Dreamers after you." The Legacy weren't her favorite people, but she didn't want to see them murdered. "This is between you and me. Leave them out of it."

"This has everything to do with them!" Dannen shrieked. She faced the cage. "You made my life miserable; treated my mother and me llike lowly servants. Always looking down your noses at us. Did you even care when she died? When I died?" She banged on the bars.

Still the women never spoke. They continued to stare at Dannen with a haughty countenance. Astrid could tell Dannen meant nothing to them.

"Nothing to say, huh. Not an ounce of remorse?" Dannnen pulled the daggers strapped to her thighs. "Well, I have no remorse about this!" She hurled them at the women, impaling two of them in the chest. Blood gushed before they collasped in a heap.

"No!" Astrid hurled herself at Dannen, daggers at the ready. With all the force she could muster, she rammed the sharp steel into Dannen's chest.

Astrid couldn't help the rush of satisfaction at the feel of her blade piercing the flesh and bone of the woman she had come to despise. She pushed the blade to the hilt and turned just for good measure.

Dannen laughed at Astrid's futile blow. "That doesn't work on me, you idiot. I'm Lespri." She grabbed Astrid's wrist and pushed her away, then pulled the knife from her chest.

Damn. She'd forgotten the rules didn't apply to Dannen anymore. Astrid knew there was no way she was going to seperate her from her head wothout her sword.

"Don't even think about that stupid sword of yours," Dannen taunted. "The only one that can kill me is a Lespri soldier. And that ain't you, honey."

Dannen flashed out of sight and into the cage housing the Legacy members. She retrieved her daggers from the two dead women, and cut the throat of the third.

She tossed a malicious smile at Astrid. "Your boyfriend's next."

She disappeared and reappeared behind Astrid and slit her throat.

CHAPTER 16

"**W**e've got to do something!" Lucien held his hands over Astrid's chest, the burning in them almost unbearable. "It's not working."

Kalyste kneeled next to him and placed her hands over his. "Let me help you. I'll enhance your healing power."

Astrid gasped and bolted upright, swinging, her fist connecting with Lucien's face.

He fell back, his hand covering his throbbing eye. "What the hell?"

Astrid jumped from the carpet, wide-eyed. "What happened? How'd I get back?"

"What do you mean, how'd you get back? You tell us. You almost died," grumbled Lucien, still cradling his eye.

"That's impossible. You can't heal the dead, and I can't rejoin my body in a person's presence."

"Technically, you weren't dead yet, and you need to forget everything you think you know," Kalyste interjected. "You aren't dealing with humans or Dreamers."

Astrid set to pacing. "She killed three Legacy members."

Lucien's head jerked up. "She what! How the hell did she get them? Are you sure they were Legacy?"

"That's what she said." Astrid pulled the elastic band from her hair, releasing the afro puff on top, and fluffed it out with her fingers. "Since no one knows who they are, I couldn't be sure she was telling the truth,, but they had the bearing of Legacy."

Lucien let out a llow whistle. "If that girl can get to them, what's to stop her from getting to us?"

Astrid sighed. "I saw five Lespri working with her."

"You saw five, but the count is a lot more," Richard replied. "A few dozen Lespri are unaccounted for at Haven. I'm hoping our contact on the inside of her little group hasn't double crossed us. Nikolai was supposed to keep this house shielded until his fake death tomorrow night. We haven't been able to contact him."

"You think she got him to join her?" Lucien jerked back when Kalyste put her hand over his eye.

"Stay still." Kalyste smiled at him. "You're going to love this."

He tried not to move despite the heat building up in his palm and eye.

"I'm sure she wouldn't get him to help her. She hates men. Her father being an asshole and being at war with Catchers all her life hasn't exactly endeared her to them. I'm afraid she may have killed him." Kalyste took her hand from Lucien's face. "How's that feel?"

He touched the once tender spot and widened his eyes. "Wow. No pain. How many powers do you have?"

Kalyste chuckled. "Thirty-nine."

Astrid abruptly stopped pacing. "Get the fuck outta here! No shit?"

She ignored Astrid's outburst. "All twelve Oracles in Haven do. Would you believe healing others isn't one of them?"

Lucien quirked a brow. "Then how did you heal me?"

"I didn't. Although you can't heal yourself, I enhanced your healing power so that you could. I can enhance or share in any power. My *aktivateur* power. When I first got it, it freaked me out. Over the years, I've learned to master it."

Lucien stood and leaned against the wall, his arms folded in front of him. "Shit, lady. With that many powers, shouldn't you be able to tap in and beat the shit out of that psycho after us?"

"Nope. I can use the three powers that are uniquely mine simultaneously, but I can't use more than one of the other thirty-three at a time, our shared powers don't work that way."

Lucien cocked his head to the side. "So, you have three powers that would be yours even if you weren't an Oracle? What are your other two?"

"Telekinesis and levitation. I don't think they're going to be of much use right now. Besides, as an Oracle, I can't do anything to Dannen. Only a Lespri soldier can kill her."

"Man," Lucien threw his hand in the air. "I've said it before, and I'll say it again. What kind of bull shit place is Haven?"

"It's what you make it." Kalyste looked to Astrid. "What do you think would happen if the Oracles had no rules? If we had absolute power with no consequences?"

Astrid nodded. It was the same question she'd asked herself when she was offered a position with the Legacy. They had no rules. "Absolute corruption."

Kalyste smiled. "It takes a woman to get it."

"Hey!" Lucien exclaimed in mock protest. He stroked his chin. "So, whose protecting us now?"

"Force field generation is one of my shared powers." Kalyste interjected. "But as long as I use it to keep Dannen out, I can't use any of my other shared powers. And none the other Oracles can interfere at this point."

Astrid plopped down on the couch in the sitting area of her room. "Our biggest problem is we've tipped our hand to Dannen. I don't think we can take her unhinged mind as a reason to underestimate her. She was cunning enough to use my face when she attacked so none of you would know who was who."

"I don't see how we tipped our hand. She knew Richard would be here. It's his responsibility to end her," Kalyste said.

Astrid's lips spread in a sly smile. "The five Lespri working with her." She turned to Kalyste. "She told me what some of their powers were. If I can identify the others, you would know what other powers we're

dealing with, right?"

"Sure. Two are working with us, but one, Nicolette, has loyalty that is questionable at best."

"What's her power?" Lucien asked.

"Invisibility." Kalyste gnawed on her lower lip. "Nicolette's judgement can be...misplaced, but she's not stupid. She's been on the straight and narrow with the Oracles since our incident few years ago."

Lucien ran a finger under his lip. "Are you sure it was Dannen who took your guy out? You said this woman, Nicollette may not be trustworthy."

"It could be anyone. All I know is that shield wasn't supposed to come down until we were ready, and we can't find him. Either Nicollette double crossed us, or Dannen has figured out what we're up to."

"To be honest, *I'm* not sure what we're up to." Astrid ran her hands through her hair. "Lucien and I were supposed to be bait, but I end up fighting alone, and witnessing the death of three Legacy members. What's to keep that from happening again?"

"Me." Lucien sidled up next to her. "Next time, she'll have to get through me."

Astrid raised her brows. "Really? Since when were you appointed my protector?"

"I wasn't appointed. I'm volunteering for the job. Besides, she's after me too. We'll protect each other." He couldn't help but think about how his heart hurt when he thought he couldn't save her. His vision of the coffin flashed in his nind. *Not on my watch.*

Her smile lit up her face. "You've got yourself a deal, mister."

CHAPTER 17

Astrid descended the creaky wooden steps leading to the gym in Lucien's basement. She was keenly aware of him following, could almost feel his body heat at her back. "When we said we'd have each other's back, I didn't mean for you to take it literally."

"This isn't just to protect you. I miss my evening workouts. I'm hoping this will help me sleep and work up an appetite. This is the wrong time to start unhealthy habits."

At the bottom of the stairs, he pulled his t-shirt off.

Astrid tried not to stare at his muscle laden chest and abdomen. "Since when do you work out topless?"

"I've always worked out this way. I wore a sweatsuit our last sessions to keep you from being uncomfortable." He smiled mischievously, white teeth and dimples drawing her gaze to his mouth. "But now that you've seen me naked, I figured the coy act would be ridiculous."

"Suit yourself." She tried to pretend he didn't faze her, but good Lord, all she wanted to do was run her tongue down his body and test his limits.

Still smiling, he sighed and rolled his eyes. "If it would make you feel better, you can take your shirt off too."

The laugh that bubbled in her throat and spilled from her lips was uncontrollable. "I'm glad you have a sense of humor, even when shit is this real."

She removed the towel from around her neck and wiped her hands. Bending from her waist, she touched her toes, breathing with the stretch, releasing tension with the expulsion of air.

Crouching slow, she extended one leg to the side and then the other until both were equally stretched wide, then leaned forward, arms extended, palms down until her groin met with the hardwood floor. Clearing her mind, she stayed in this position, concentrating on her breath and freeing herself of stress.

The sound of metal meeting metal reminded her she wasn't alone, and she straightened, her legs still spread on either side of her. She looked up to see Lucien seated at a workout machine, pulling down on the mechanical bars, the weight clanking with every rep.

"How much weight you got on there?" Astrid couldn't tear her gaze from the rippling muscles in his arms and chest.

His full lips spread in that damned sexy, come do me smile. "Want to use the machine?"

Astrid hopped from her position and straightened. "Don't stop on my account. There are plenty of other machines I can use."

She straddled a bench and added weight to the bottom bar. Leaning forward, she repeated some arm curls, continuing to study his sexy form. "Can I ask you a question?" She tried to keep her tone casual.

Not giving him a chance to answer, she went on. "What did I do to piss you off earlier? I was trying to offer you comfort, and you stalked off like I had just made a bad your mamma joke."

He replaced his weights to their original position and strode toward her.

Astrid unconsciously licked her lips, and inhaled, hoping he didn't hear it.

"Your form is a little off." He sat behind her on the bench and snaked an arm around her waist, lightly pressing his palm against her belly. "Straighten your spine and pull your center up."

His spicy scent enveloped her. The response of her body being pressed against his made her grateful she was sitting down. She wasn't sure her legs would support her. "I know how to do this. I've been doing it for years." Knowing the tremor in her voice betrayed her desire, she gave in to making sure they moved toward a better, more pleasurable workout. She lifted his hand from her stomach and kissed it, then turned her head to the side and inhaled his scent.

"What do you want, Astrid?" His deep voice vibrated against her ear as he ran his hand down her thigh.

"I want you. Right now. I'm not asking for forever, or even the entire night. I'm asking for right here, now. Can you give me that?"

He lifted her from the bench carried her to a mat on the other side of the gym. He covered her with his body taking care not to put all his weight on her.

"You're sure?" He traced her lips with his thumb.

She couldn't find her voice to say the words, could only nod, and lifted her face to his, meeting his lips for a hungry kiss.

His tongue tangled with hers, slick and gliding, exploring her mouth. He pushed her sports bra up and over her head. His hands trailed down to her breasts, brushing both nipples with his thumbs.

The tingles from her breasts to her pussy were almost unbearable. She ran her hands down his back to the waistband of his sweatpants and jerked them down to uncover his ass. She replaced the material with her hands, running them over the smooth, muscled surface.

He tugged them off the rest of the way with his shoes and socks stuck in the pant legs. His gaze never left hers as he removed her pants.

Butterfly kisses covered her neck and chest until he got to her breast and drew a nipple into his warm mouth.

Astrid cradled his head, taking care to savor every moment, every sensation, letting go of all inhibitions.

He took her hands in his and trailed kisses down her body, stopping at her pussy. He lightly blew on her clit and touched the tip with his wet tongue.

Astrid didn't think she could take the anticipation anymore. She lifted her butt off the mat, attempting to meet his mouth. If he let go of her hands, she would hold his head down there until she was satisfied.

When he finally buried his face in her pussy, she thought she would fly of the mat and hit the ceiling. His tongue delved inside her, then in low tantalizing circles on and round her clit. Astrid came in waves, her body quaking and shivering.

Lucien slid back up her body his face hovering over hers. She pulled his head to her, their lips meeting in a long, lingering kiss. Her taste and scent on his lips made her stomach dip, her center throbbing, wanting to be filled.

He moved to her side, on his knees. "Turn over."

Without hesitation, Astrid turned onto her belly. Waiting, in anticipation. His lips and tongue explored the center of her back and up to her neck, his warm breath tickling her ear.

"Are you ready for me?" he murmured.

"Yes." The word traveled on a soft moan.

Lucien positioned himself between her legs and placed his hand on her waist. Gently, he urged her hips up until she was on her knees, the lower half of her body still flat against the mat.

He plunged into her.

Stroking her slow and deep. He reached around and played with her clit, never breaking his rhythm.

Sliding his hands between her and the mat, he lifted her upper body to settle back against him, his dick never losing contact with her pussy.

Astrid took control of the pace. She rode him fast and hard. His dick surged and jerked inside her. She tightened her muscles, circling and edging her own climax.

Moans and screams sounded far away, but she didn't realize they were her own until she felt the rawness in her throat. "Lucien!" His name burst from her lips and she came, her body exploding in pleasure.

Repeating her name over and over, he held her up against his chest as he reached his own release.

They collapsed, and without a word, fell asleep right there on the floor, Astrid wrapped in his arms.

CHAPTER 18

L ucien stretched and yawned. He rolled over and spooned Astrid, inhaling the scent of coconut in her hair. His dick stirred with thoughts of the night before.

After dozing off on the gym floor, he and Astrid retired to his room. The next few hours were filled with them getting to know every inch of each other's body.

He gazed down at her, listening to her deep breathing. Fate was a mean bitch. The only thing he wanted right now was to forget their lives were in danger, and spend the day wearing out his mattress.

Brushing a lock of hair from her face, he kissed her neck. "Wake up, baby. We've got a lot to do."

Barely opening an eye, she groaned and turned to face him nuzzling her nose to his chest. "I don't want to fight bad guys today." She pulled the blanket over her head. "Let's stay here."

"Sorry, no can do," he said, yanking the covers off them.

"Spoil sport." She rose from the bed and sauntered toward the bathroom, her naked body highlighted by the sun peeking through the curtains. Stopping to look back, she licked her lips. "You coming?"

That was all the invitation he needed. He followed behind her and pulled two bath towels from the linen closet, setting them on a stool outside the enormous walk-in shower.

Warm water sprayed from the two nozzles in each wall, and the rain showerhead suspended from the ceiling.

Astrid stepped in and closed her eyes, the water cascading down her body, pure bliss on her face.

Lucien stepped in behind her and picked up a sponge and soap from the rack mounted on the wall. He soaped her neck, sliding the sponge across her back and butt, down her legs. "Turn around."

Astrid did as she was told and allowed him to wash her front, inhaling sharply when he touched her center.

She took the sponge from him and put it back in its place on the rack. Her palms slid across his chest and over his stomach resting on his dick. Firmly massaging and stroking, she dropped to her knees on the warm, smooth stone floor and took him in her mouth.

Lucien glanced down, his breath catching in his throat at the sight of her sucking him off. Her one hand palmed the base of his dick while the other played with the opening around his asshole. His toes curled at the foreign sensation setting off tingles and shockwaves throughout his body.

Waves of pleasure washed over him, his breathing becoming erratic gasps. His muscled tightened and he groaned loudly.

"Oh shit!" he yelled, before he found his release. She kept his dick enclosed in her warm mouth, never breaking suction, until he was well spent.

He sagged against the wall, holding onto one of the shower shelves for support. "Damn, woman. The things you can do with your mouth and hands are fucking fantastic." Lucien concentrated on steadying his breathing and galloping heart rate.

She rose, her hands gliding over his water slicked skin and kissed him lightly on the chin. "Come on, baby. Let's go get us some bad guys."

***

"I say we take the fight to her." Astrid sat on the edge of the desk in Lucien's library. The one thing she wanted more than anything was to get that bitch dealt with. "She can't beat me in a fair fight. That popping in and out of sight thing is the only thorn in my side."

"It's a big enough thorn to get you killed," Kalyste replied. "And you know she doesn't care about a fair fight."

Astrid glanced at Lucien. "But if your dad is there, he can do his thing and save the day."

Kalyste shot that suggestion down before Lucien had a chance to answer. "He'll be there, but how do we make her come to us on our terms? Sure, we could drop the force field, but we still wouldn't know when she would show."

Jazz music blared from Lucien's phone. He glanced at the screen. "It's Enoch at the Catcher station." He put the phone on speaker and placed it next to him. "What's up, E? Got you on speaker and everyone's here."

"Man, you need to get your asses here right now! She found the station. Had some women with her that makes the Legacy look like a bunch of helpless old women on walkers. You should see this place. Somiar and Malachi have gone down the rabbit hole after your girl. She's got the kids."

Before Lucien could respond, they were all were at the Catcher station, standing next to Enoch in the infirmary.

"Teleporter." Kalyste answered the question before Enoch could ask.

Several injured and severely wounded Catchers were being sorted and treated according to the severity of their condition. Somiar and Malachi were on a gurney, both unconscious.

Enoch examined the telemetry monitors connected to the couple. "They used stardust. I assume they're together. Hopefully, Somiar pulled him to her. She can track the kids, but I don't want them in there alone."

"What the hell happened?" Lucien peered at the cameras in the main quarters and halls of the Catcher station. Pieces of broken equipment and papers littered the floors. Blood smeared the walls. Lights flickered in some sections. Catchers were dispatched to various areas put out small electrical fires. "It looks like a war zone."

"There was definitely a war going on." Enoch's jaw clenched, the muscles twitching. "Craziest shit I ever saw. Hundreds of women just...appeared. Don't know where the hell they came from. Sort of like what you just did. Shit flying all over the place. Jaden is dead."

"What!" Lucien snapped his head up. "How?"

"One of those crazy bitches stuck her hand right through his chest. Just reached in like he wasn't solid, and pulled his heart out. Another of our men went up in flames. Bobcats and tigers attacked then disappeared. I made it to the main quarters to make sure the kids were okay. Malachi and Somiar were in the hall fighting air. No one was there. They swore they'd just seen someone."

"The chaos was definitely to keep all of you busy while they kidnapped the children." Kalyste wiped her eyes, tears staining her cheeks. "Those Lespri who killed and assisted Dannen have forfeited their lives. They are my people, and they will die."

***

Rage enveloped Lucien like a shroud. He clenched his fist at his sides until his nails bit into his palms. "As they should. These men are like family to me. Brothers. And now two of *my* people are dead."

Kalyste stiffened her spine and sniffed. "We don't know who they are yet, but we know what powers they have."

Astrid cocked her head. "If you know what their powers are, why don't you know who they are?"

"Because more than one person in Haven can have the same power. All we know is that they are female and there were seven here, not hundreds." Kalyste nibbled on her lip.

"One." She held up a finger. "Is an illusionist. That's why you thought there were hundreds of them. Next." She held up another finger. "Has the power of telekinesis. Third." Another finger up. "Conjuror. That's were all the animals came from. Four," Kalyste lowered her hand and her head. "Four was a wall walker. They can walk through solid matter, and that's usually all they do. This one used her hand to go through your friend and kill him. Five was a fire starter. She killed your other man."

"Dannen makes six," Astrid supplied. "Who was number seven?"

"Nicolette. She was probably the one who was fighting Somiar and Malachi. She has the power of invisibility. That's why you couldn't see her. The bitch double crossed us. She led them away from the children so Dannen could take them."

Lucien ran a shaky hand over his head. "Astrid, can you track them?"

She shook her head. "No. That was a skill I never learned. It's taught only if you become a Legacy member. I don't know how Somiar is doing it."

"We can do a lot of things our peers can't because of our parentage."
Lucien settled into a chair. "I can see through Somiar's eyes. Maybe
I can get a read on where they are. Unfortunately, that'll render her
blind, and unable to heal. If I do that at the wrong time, it could mean
her life."

Astrid rubbed the back of her neck. "Give me the stardust."

"What?" Lucien furrowed his brow.

"The stardust. Give it to me. If she took them to the same place we
were before, maybe I can find her."

"You said you were in a cave. Do you know how many caves there
are in the world?"

"That's not such a bad idea." Kalyste came to stand in front of
them. "But you can't take the stardust yet. Dannen made a big mistake
taking the children. One of the powers I share is summoning, I can
summon anyone to any place or send them anywhere."

Lucien stared at her opened mouthed. "If you can do that, why the
hell have we been chasing our tails all this time?" He took a breath,
reminding himself that he was shouting at one of the people on their
side. Bringing his tone down a notch, he continued. "Why didn't you
just summon that crazy bitch to you with my dad on stand-by so he
could give her the ax?"

Kalyste arched her brows and held up a hand. "Don't you think
we've tried that?" She rolled her neck and continued. "Some of our
powers don't work on Dannen. We think it's because she's a Dreamer
and Lespri. It's one of the reasons Richard has never been able to track
her. If she were just Lespri, this would have been over rather quickly
and I would have never been involved. I told you. This is something
we've never had to deal with before."

Kalyste raked Lucien over from head to toe, and with an eye roll,
turned her back on him, letting him know she was clearly done arguing

with him. Instead, she addressed Astrid. "I don't know if I can send you to the children as a Dreamer. But I know I can in your human body."

"Hold on," Lucien interrupted. "Why don't you just summon the kids back here?"

"I can, but then, I couldn't use them as a beacon anymore. We'd have no clue how to find Dannen."

"Fuck that!" Lucien threw his hands in the air. "They're children for fuck's sake! Astrid and I agreed to be bait, no-one said anything about the kids."

Kalyste slammed her hand on the table. "Calm yourself! Malachi and Somiar went for the children. If I took them, they would be roaming around enemy territory looking for children that aren't there."

"Send me to them." Astrid's husky voice cut the crackling tension in the air.

"I said I would go," Lucien ground out. "There's no way I'll allow you to go."

Astrid jerked around to face Lucien. "I know you mean well, but screw you, dude. I'm not helpless, and you don't get to tell me what to do."

Enoch tapped Lucien on the shoulder. "Can ya'll argue about this later? We've got to get all of them out of there. No telling what Somiar and Malachi are walking into."

Until that point, Enoch had been so quiet, Lucien forgot he was in the room. "Why don't you send all of us?"

Kalyste tapped her lip with her forefinger. She turned to Enoch. "You want to go too?"

"Mal and Somiar are my best friends and I love those babies. You bet your ass I'm going." Enoch cracked his knuckles. "Ready when you are."

"Never used my summoning power on a whole group before." Kalyste closed her eyes. "Just give me a sec to get a read on the kids."

A low hum filled the room. Her hair lifted from her shoulders as if being toyed with by unseen fingers. "Hold on to your drawers, everyone. We're about to enter the land of crazy."

"We arrived there a long time ago," Lucien scoffed.

CHAPTER 19

Astrid squinted against the bright sunlight peeking through the trees. Her group were shoulder to shoulder, surrounded by dense foliage and trees. Birds and animals created a wild symphony of sound.

Lucien looked around, his gaze resting on Kalyste. "You sure this is the place?"

Kalyste nodded. "This is where my summoning power led me. They have to be within a two-mile radius."

Lucien motioned to his friend. "Enoch, give Astrid the stardust."

Enoch pulled the glass vial filled with blue liquid from his pocket and handed it to Astrid.

She downed the contents, trying not to gag when the bitter taste assaulted her tongue. Everything blurred. Colors collided like a child's fingerpainting. Her legs no longer supported her. She resisted the natural urge to fight the heavy drowsiness dulling her senses.

The potent scent of earth and grass permeated her nostrils. The sky was a clear, baby blue. No trees blocking her view. The sound of rushing water told her a brook was nearby.

She sat up, trying to figure out where she was. The forest ringed the small clearing. Her comrades were nowhere in sight. Closing her eyes, she listened intently to the sounds of the forest.

Voices. Barely perceptible voices. She crept toward the them, paying close attention to the placement of her feet, so as not make a sound that would alert anyone of her presence. She couldn't be sure the voices she heard were her friends. She exhaled the breath she was holding when she saw her crew.

Enoch's ring glowed at her appearance.

Lucien nudged him. "You might want to douse that light. We don't want to tip anyone off that we're here."

Enoch tore off a piece of his shirt and wrapped it around his finger, concealing his ring.

Astrid quirked a brow. "Wouldn't it be easier to take it off?"

He scowled at her, as if she'd said something offensive. "This ring means something to me. A symbol of brotherhood. And I don't take it off for anyone."

"Wow, stardust is some heavy-duty shit," Kalyste whispered. She turned to address Lucien. "You mind telling me who's going to stay out here and guard her body while we're all in there?"

Lucien stroked his chin. "Enoch, would you mind?"

"How's he going to protect her if more than one of them show up?" Kalyste put her hands on her hips. "He has no powers. At least on the inside, I can enhance his fighting skills. I can't do shit if I can't see him."

"Can't you send her body someplace safe?" Lucien's clipped tone made Astrid raise a brow.

She put her hand in his and locked gazes with him. "We're going to get your family back."

A smug smile spread Kalyste's lips. "I know just the spot." Kneeling next to Astrid's body, she placed her hand in Astrid's limp palm, her body disappearing.

She glared at Kalyste. "Hey! What happened to my body?"

"It's at Haven." Kalyste pursed her lips. "Or rather, right outside Haven."

"What! Are you trying to tell me I'm dead?"

"No, you're not dead. I didn't say you were *in* Haven. Just close enough for the Oracles to guard you. But be warned, there is no special treatment. If you die here, your body dies there. They aren't allowed to save you. But because of your body's close proximity to Haven, they're allowed to keep any Lespri from attacking your human body."

"Gee, thanks. My human body thanks you."

Lucien rubbed his hands together. "I think it's time we go and get this done."

He glanced at Astrid. "You see anything where you arrived?"

She shook her head. "A stream, other than that, nothing but trees and wildlife. No signs of civilization."

Lucien sighed. "Well, if Somiar is anywhere around, I can't sense her. The only Dreamer I'm sensing is you."

Astrid frowned. "You're not wearing a Catcher's ring. How can you sense me?"

Lucien gave her a withering look. "Now's not the time."

Astrid didn't press the issue. He was right. They had to focus on their task.

"I'll take a look and see if I can get a lay of the land." Kalyste snapped her fingers and her clothes changed into the camouflaged pattern of a military uniform. Taking care to stay in the tangle of forest foliage, she rose among the branches to the treetops, her body slowly rotating.

"Now there's something you don't see every day," Astrid mumbled.

They patiently waited for her to finish her survey and return to them.

"There's a house about a mile out. Or should I say mansion? The damned thing looks deserted, and creepy as hell, but I'm pretty sure that's where Dannen and her crew are. It's the only explanation for my summoning power bringing us here."

Lucien rubbed his forehead. "Wait. Is the house gray, a tall stone wall surrounding it, with a huge lion statue in front?"

"You know where we are?" Kalyste drew her brows together.

"Yeah. Somiar's adoptive monster owned this house. She's been trying to unload it for years, but no one wants to live in Romania in the middle of nowhere."

Astrid's mouth dropped open. "Romania! No shit?"

"I've only been here once, about a year ago. Mal and I came here with Somiar to see what condition the place was in. It's been neglected, but it'll serve Dannen's purpose. It even has a dungeon carved into the mountain."

Astrid snapped her fingers. "The cave. I wonder why she chose Somiar's home?"

Richard joined their ranks. "Because it belonged to a Legacy member. She hates them. This is a trophy for her. And, it's the last place any of us would look."

"Hey." Lucien barely acknowledged his father before turning away.

"Son."

He inclined his head toward Astrid. "Astrid."

He turned to Enoch, whose face seemed to be frozen in shock. "It's alright, brother. It's really me."

"Shit! Richard!" Enoch almost knocked Richard over with the force of his hug. "You don't know how much I've missed you, man. You're alive."

"Well, not really, but we have more important things to discuss. We're in for the fight of our life." He addressed everyone. "Remember, I'm the only one who can kill Dannen. She's *my* rogue."

"Got it," Lucien said. "Kalyste is going to have to lead the way to the house. I've never had to hike there in this forest, so I don't know where it is from here. Listen." He touched Richard's arm. "She has the kids, and Somiar is in there somewhere."

"We're going to get them back son. And Dannen will die."

***

Astrid watched father and son as they strode along in hushed conversation. A pang of jealousy nudged her. She wished she'd known her father and loved her mother more than she did before she died.

As they got closer to the house, the group continued in silence, everyone alert, taking care to make as little noise as possible in the crunching leaves.

They came to the cave at the base of the mountain. "How far back does this go?" Astrid whispered and touched Lucien's hand.

"Several hundred feet. The cells are carved into the walls, with heavy iron doors."

She inched along the wall behind him, barely breathing, praying everyone was still alive. When they rounded the corner, Astrid couldn't believe her eyes. The children were limp in one cell, their bodies covered in blood. Gaping wounds in their necks gushed.

"No!" Lucien darted to the cell and kneeled next to Ruby. He held her close, her body flopping like a rag-doll.

A dark-skinned woman appeared in the center of the room. She was tall, her black hair flowing to her waist. Ebony eyes took in the intruders in the room. She gazed toward the cell where Lucien sat, still holding his niece.

"Nicolette," Kalyste hissed. She thrust out her hand, sending Nicolette hurtling through the air, landing against a stone wall. "How could you do this?" Another blast sent Nicolette to the opposite wall.

Nicolette got to her hands and knees and held up a hand. "Wait. I didn't. What's happening?"

"You've betrayed us for the last time, bitch." Kalyste hurled her into one of the empty cages and willed the door shut. Again, holding out her hand she watched as Nicolette slumped on the dirt floor.

"What are you doing?" Nicolette cried. "I don't understand what's happening."

"I've drained your powers. You can't hurt anyone else. I'm taking you back to Haven and you will die for this."

Nicolette again looked helplessly at the cage. "I didn't do this! I did everything you asked."

Astrid kneeled next to Lucien. "I'm so sorry, baby." Blind fury heated her face as she watched Nicolette crawl across her cell. What kind of monster would kill a child?

Her hair stood on end and her spine tingled. Something was wrong. She went and examined Lucien's two nephews. Their small bodies were cold, but they felt waxy. She lifted one boy's closed eyelid. Empty sockets. "Oh, my God," she gasped. "Lucien, put her down. Back away."

As soon as the words were out of her mouth, the boys disappeared and the female child Lucien was holding shapeshifted to Dannen. Before he could fling her away, she plunged her long dagger into his chest.

"No!" Astrid screamed making her way to where Lucien lay. She whirled around in time to see Dannen racing toward her, sword raised.

In a lightning-fast move, Astrid unsheathed her sword and blocked Dannen's blow. She lunged at Dannen, forcing her back until they were out of the confines of the cell. Richard came up behind Dannen, preparing to deliver the final blow.

Four more women materialized, one with a hand directed at Richard, who immediately caught fire. He dropped to the ground and rolled, putting himself out, then charged at the woman who'd set him ablaze.

The interruption was enough to catch Dannen off guard. Astrid plunged her sword straight through Dannen's chest until it went through her back.

Dannen flashed an evil smile as she pulled the sword from her chest and the wound healed. "You fool," Dannen laughed. "That doesn't work on me. And I'll have to remember to thank Kalyste for handling that two faced bitch." She quickly smirked at Nicolette then returned her attention to Astrid. "Saved me the trouble." Dannen tossed Astrid's sword into a far cell, well out of reach.

Astrid pulled her long daggers from the sheaths strapped to her thighs and threw one at Dannen, aiming for her head. In a blink, Dannen disappeared.

The sharp pain in her back took her breath away. She fell to her knees and pitched forward. Another pain, and her body jerked.

Dannen's laugh sounded far off. "I wish I could have seen your face when my sword pierced your flesh. You've lost. Now, watch as your friends die." Dannen hauled Astrid to her feet, and slammed her against the stone wall. She used her long dagger and drove it into her shoulder, pinning her in place.

Richard charged Dannen, but she turned in time to see him coming. She blocked the blow and countered with one of her own. She disappeared and reappeared at different points in the cave, Richard in pursuit.

The clang and chaos of war was deafening. Through her pain, Astrid took in the carnage.

She caught sight of Enoch fighting with an Amazon of a woman. She towered over him, but he was holding his own.

Another woman, dressed in the same black and red garb as Richard, materialized behind his foe, and manifested a sword. With a single blow, she decapitated his enemy.

I have to get away. Astrid scanned the room, searching for Kalyste. She hadn't seen her since the fighting started. They were getting their asses handed to them and Kalyste was nowhere to be found. She looked to where Lucien lay motionless, and tried to slow her racing heart. *I refuse to die this way.*

The ground rumbled. A loud roar shook the cave. Loose rocks fell from the ceiling and walls. Out of nowhere, a giant dragon appeared in the middle of the room.

Astrid felt her eyes grow wide at the sight. Did someone slip something in her morning coffee? What kind of acid trip was this?

All the fighting stopped. She cast her gaze to the woman standing between the dragon's feet, her eyes closed, flaming red hair stirring and swirling around her.

The conjuror. Despite her horror, Astrid couldn't help being impressed. *Now that's a cool power.*

Dannen cackled. "Looks like playtime is over. Say good-bye everyone."

The dragon roared, his hot breath heating the entire cavern.

Astrid closed her eyes, waiting for oblivion. When it didn't come, she opened one eye, then the other, and didn't trust what she saw.

The dragon was gone. The woman who had been standing between his feet, lay limp on the dirt floor, her head several feet away. Another woman stood in her place, wearing the same black and red uniform Richard wore, a blood-streaked sword in her hand.

Two men and another woman stood behind the other three Rogue Lespri, all wearing the black and red soldier uniforms, swords raised.

"Guilty!" A booming, but feminine, disembodied voice rang throughout the cavern.

With one blow, each Lespri soldier decapitated their charge. With a slight nod, the soldiers and their victims, faded from sight.

Kalyste ran to Astrid and, with a motion of her hand, freed the daggers that kept her pinned.

Astrid fell to the ground. "Lucien. We have to get to Lucien. He's not doing well." She silently prayed he was okay.

***

Kalyste held Astrid to her as they floated across the cavern to where Lucien lay.

He was still unconscious and sweating. A pool of blood soaked into the dirt ground below.

Astrid felt for his pulse. "It's slow and thready." She looked up at Kalyste. "He's dying. Help him. Heal him."

"I can't. It's not one of my powers, and he's not strong enough to help me strengthen his healing power." She gazed at Astrid, concern etched in her beautiful features. "You don't look so good yourself. You should get back to your human body. I can't heal you either."

"You can't, but we have someone who can." Somiar's voice came from behind Kalyste.

Astrid craned her neck to see Somiar and Malachi, along with their children. Somiar led one boy to Lucien, their daughter tightly clutching her other hand. Malachi led the other boy to her. The boys placed their tiny hands on the wounds.

"They're young. They may need some help," Malachi addressed Kalyste.

She covered their hands with hers and closed her eyes. "I'll absorb the heat so the boys don't burn their hands." Kalyste clenched her teeth.

The blood disappeared from Astrid's clothes and from the ground where Lucien lay.

He sat up and rubbed the back of his head. "What happened?" Tears poured from his eyes when he saw the triplets. "They're alive." He scurried across the ground to embrace them. "They're alive!"

Astrid sat back and watched the four of them. She welcomed Lucien's arms around her once he let the children go.

Enoch rushed into the cell. "Thank God, you all are okay." He gathered the children to him.

"Uncle E, you're squishing us," Ruby squealed and laughed. "Mommy, we're ready to go home. We don't like it here."

Her brothers nodded in agreement.

"I can send them to the Catcher station." Kalyste said. She glanced at Enoch. "Can you take them somewhere safe once I send you back? I have to speak to their folks."

"Sure, I got it covered."

Kalyste nodded and with a wave of her hand, they were gone. She turned back to the group. "Dannen got away, but Richard is hot on her trail. She'll have trouble finding anyone else to join her cause now that some of her accomplices have been delivered the final death."

"Yeah," Astrid said. "I'd hate to be on the bad side of the booming voice from hell." Giving Kalyste a sidelong stare, she nibbled on her lower lip. "Care to share what the heck that was all about?"

Kalyste laughed. "That was Ella. She's a judge at Haven. Since this was a mass final death delivery, she was letting us know it was being recorded as justified. Sort of like a certified record that they all had it coming."

Astrid motioned to Nicolette, still weeping on the ground in the next cell. "What happens to her?"

"Oh, no!" Somiar pulled on the heavy cell door, and with Malachi's help, pulled it open. "You didn't hurt her, did you?" She knelt next to the trembling woman.

"Why are you concerned for the woman who tried to kill your children? She betrayed us," Kalyste ground out.

"No, she didn't," Malachi corrected. "She was the one who led us to them. When we saw her at the Catcher station, we assumed the worst. She tried to warn us that Dannen was in the building, but we attacked her before she could get a word out. She used her invisibility power so we'd have no other choice but to listen to her."

"It's true." Somiar helped Nicolette from the dirt floor. "Whatever you did to her, you need to reverse." She guided her to Kalyste.

"Once I took the stardust and pulled Malachi in, she led us here. The kids were in the master quarters on the third floor." Somiar rubbed her arms. "I always hated this place. This just reinforces my opinion."

Kalyste bit her lip. "I'm so sorry, Nicolette." She waved a hand over Nicolette's head. "I don't know how to repay you for what you've done, and make amends for the way I've treated you today."

"I know I've done some questionable things in the past." Nicolette looked away. "But what have I ever done to make you think I'd stoop to murdering innocent children? To murdering anyone for that matter?"

Kalyste had never felt like such a lowlife. She'd let her personal issues with Nicolette cloud her judgement. As an Oracle, she should have known better. "I will find a way to make this up to you. I swear it."

Nicolette didn't acknowledge Kalyste's apology. "Rhana's dead." She glared at Lucien. "She was a friend of mine and went undercover along with me. Dannen killed her while she was trying to save *your* friend."

Kalyste inhaled sharply. "We need to get back. Nicolette, please go back to Haven. Let the Oracles know what Dannen has done."

Nicolette vanished from sight without another word.

"I'll send your body back to Lucien's house," Kalyste said to Astrid. "We'll meet you there."

"Our kids need to sleep in their own beds tonight. They've been through enough today," Malachi said.

After closing her eyes for several seconds, Malachi tapped her shoulder. "You still awake?"

Kalyste opened her eyes and met his concerned gaze. "Yes. I was communicating with the Oracles. The situation with Dannen has been elevated. They're allowing more Oracles to help, but not in the fighting. It's still Richard's responsibility to deliver her final death. They think you should stay with your children. You may take them home. Najac and Omari are two Oracles who have agreed to guard your house."

With Malachi's nod, Kalyste sent them home.

She turned to Astrid and Lucien. "We have to end this. We have three days left."

"I think I know how," Astrid replied. "I know what Dannen can't resist, but you might not like it."

CHAPTER 20

"You want us to do what?" Lucien sat back in his chair, arms crossed on the kitchen table in front of him.

"I think we need to involve the Legacy." She hurried on before he could tear down her idea. "She's already killed three of them. What's to keep her from going after the rest, and their progenies?" Astrid couldn't tell if he thought her idea was brilliant or lunacy.

"Yeah, I heard you the first time. I'm just making sure I heard you right." Lucien shook his head. "We can't trust them. They've been hunting Catchers for decades. And you know how badly they want to see me and Somiar taken out."

He pinned Kalyste with a glare. "Does this sound like a good idea to you?"

"Actually, it does." She crossed the room to address Astrid. "The problem is, if they turn on you, we can't kill any of them. I may be an Oracle, but I have to abide by the same rules as any other Lespri. Kill no Lespri who are not my rogue, harm no human. The Legacy may have supernatural powers, but they are still human."

"Understood," Astrid said. "They won't turn on us. They aren't totally without a moral code. After all is done, you can have their memories wiped of all knowledge of the Lespri."

"Definitely," Lucien concurred. "Their knowledge of you is the last thing we need. No telling what kind of crap they'd try to pull after this is over," he scoffed. "Look at all the chaos just one started. And she's a low-level Dreamer." He furrowed his brow. "I wish there was a way to do this without letting them know about you."

"It can't be helped," Astrid sighed. "How else do we explain to them that a long dead Dreamer killed three of their members? If we're not careful, she might proclaim herself to be some sort of god and recruit Dreamers to her cause."

"You really think it could come to that?" Lucien stroked his chin and glanced at Kalyste.

"I guess it's possible. If she could sway some of our people, there's no reason she wouldn't be able to turn some Dreamers."

"Especially the ones on the low level of the hierarchy. It'd be an enormous boost to their ego to stick it to the Legacy," Astrid added.

Astrid slapped her hands against her thigh. "Then it's settled. I'll contact the Legacy and we can start the negotiations." She licked her lips at Lucien's suspicious glare.

Opening the fridge, she took out a bottle of water. "Oh, come on, did you think the Legacy would let me go, no questions asked, and not keep me on their radar? Why do you think someone within eyeshot of your property is always getting lawn service, satellite service or a myriad of other 'services' and they're all women? Wouldn't surprise me if they had a residence nearby."

Astrid inched closer to him and placed her palm against his face. "Don't question my loyalty. Not now. We have to trust each other."

"I've always known they were there. Even before you came along, but it never occurred to me to invite them in." He gazed into to her eyes and covered her hand in his, lowering it from his face, entwining their fingers.

"Fine, they can come here, but they'll be confined to the bottom level for the meeting." He turned to Kalyste. "I need you to reverse whatever you did to the Catcher stones to render them useless against Dreamers. The Legacy would never come in any form other than their Dreamer bodies."

Kalyste drew her brows together. "Are you sure?"

"If you had a secret identity, wouldn't you want to protect it? No one knows what the Legacy really looks like. It would be like Clark Kent showing up for a meeting meant for Superman in front of all his enemies."

"He's right. They need to be confined to one room." Astrid said.

Kalyste nodded. "Fine with me. As long as you know what the rules are."

"Give me your phone." Astrid motioned toward Lucien's phone.

"Let me guess. You have a direct line to the Legacy." Lucien leaned against the wall, his arms folded in front of him.

"Course not. I gave up that right when I left. But I still have friends in high places. They'll deliver the message."

He raised his brows and scoffed, "Not a chance in hell are you going to use my phone. I don't want the Legacy to have me on speed dial. Use the dummy phone."

Astrid put the phone on speaker, and waited for the call to connect. "Surely you know they've probably got your number already."

"Hello?" The sing-song tone of the woman on the other end of the line made Astrid smile.

Octavia was the only Dreamer who kept in touch after Astrid left the life. Always joyful and full of energy. She loved Astrid, but made it no secret that she would never betray the Dreamers, nor the Legacy. Not even for their friendship. She was a killer through and through when she had to be.

"Octavia, Astrid here. I need to get with the Legacy. Secure terminal six, six, two. And by the way, tell whoever has been watching my house to be a pal and apply some rose food to the soil in the bushes at the side of the house." Not waiting for a response, she hung up.

"We should hear something in about an hour. They're going to want to go through all the proper procedures to make sure I haven't been compromised."

"Haven't you?" Lucien shuffled his feet and fidgeted. "Sorry," he said, noticing Astrid's acerbic frown. "So, we've got an hour to kill? Maybe we can go over strategies, or something."

Astrid tossed him a wry grin. "Are you okay? What's wrong?" She almost missed the quick glance in Kalyste's direction. "What did I miss?"

Kalyste cleared her throat. "I think I'll go...um... anywhere but here." Without another word, she disappeared.

Astrid turned to Lucien, confusion wrinkling her brow. She jerked a thumb where Kalyste stood seconds ago. "What was that all about?"

"You don't know how sexy you are, do you?"

"What?" Astrid gazed at Lucien. He looked like a man who'd been picked to spend the night of his dreams with a sex kitten. "Seriously? You're turned on right now?"

"Yes, seriously. I'm turned on right now." He ran the tip of his tongue along his top lip. His eyes gleamed as he took a couple of slow, deliberate steps toward her, stopping just beyond her reach.

She could almost feel the rush of excitement coursing through him. Ah, yes. She knew this game. "Let me guess. The adrenaline junkie in you has kicked in." She narrowed her eyes, a slow smile spreading her full lips. "You get off on danger. Thrive on the tension."

It was a feeling she knew well. Her rush came after the completion of a mission. His apparently came in the middle. Circling him, she paused, taking in his perfect round ass, remembering the way the muscles tensed and relaxed under her fingers.

He waited for her to finish her survey of his body before pulling her to him. "When it comes to danger and tension, sex is the perfect yoga." He brushed her lips, then lightly tasted a route from her ear down her neck. "But danger isn't how I get off lately."

"Umm," Astrid moaned. "Dare I ask?"

"I get off on getting *you* off."

Taking a step back, she looked him up and down, trying to slow her racing pulse. The urge to rip his clothes to shreds had to be controlled with deliberate breaths. "Did you plan this with Kalyste? Is that why she left in such a hurry?"

"No." He ran his lips across her cheek, his breath warm on her skin. "She's also an empath. If she can feel what I do, she's probably fucking the shit out of her husband right now."

Astrid leaned back to look him in the eye, brows raised. "Oh, really?"

"Yes, really." He loosened his embrace. "Of course, it's your call."

"Uh-huh." She jerked at the front of his shirt, its buttons littering the floor. Teasing the tip of his exposed chest with her tongue, she savored his masculine scent. Soft hairs tickled her nose. She ran her fingers down the hard ridges of his stomach to the waistband of his pants.

He covered her hands in his. "Wait." His fingers made quick work of the closure of her jeans, before removing her socks and shoes.

She stepped out of her pants and pulled her shirt over her head. Barely freeing herself of her bra, she felt his hands grab her ass and lift her from the floor, settling her on the edge of the kitchen table.

His lips explored hers, tasting and teasing her tongue. Warm, slick, and tantalizing, she let him explore. He dropped to his knees and kissed her toes to her knees.

His warm hands caressed her thighs as he buried his face in her pussy. Astrid reclined back on her elbows. For a moment she gazed at the motion of his head between her thighs, the visual heightening her arousal. Giving in to the sensations of her body, she closed her eyes. His tongue slid across her clit like warm, slick silk. She was hot and cold at the same time. Tingles and shivers took over.

Licking her lips, she palmed his head, writhing against his mouth, not caring about anything except the pleasure of the moment.

"Lucien," she screamed, her hips convulsing.

He rose and brushed her tongue with his, her taste and scent all over him. He raised her legs and urged her flat on her back, both her legs over his shoulders. Going in deep and steady, her pussy quivered at the sensation of his thickness filling her.

She squeezed the muscles of her sex, and placed her palms against his pelvis. "Slower baby. You're a lot of man to handle in this position."

Biting his lower lip, he smiled. "Your wish is my command." Slowing his pace, he leaned back and caressed her clit with his fingers, never breaking his stroke.

Astrid thought she would fly apart from the sensation. She didn't want it to end. Lowering her legs, she locked gazes with him. "Get on your back."

He moved to the center of the table.

Astrid straddled him, and controlled the pace. Hips rolling slow and smooth, she took his length inside her, savoring every inch. Her pussy convulsed and contracted, along with her movements, soaking him with her desire.

Lucien groaned and flipped her over on her hands and knees. Faster and faster, his strokes delved deep inside her. She felt his warm palms dig into her shoulders as he rode her strong and long.

"I can't hold back anymore baby. I'm cumming!" Astrid screamed his name over and over.

Lucien covered her breasts with his palms and pulled her back against him, his dick still buried in her pussy. "Hold on just a little bit...more." The last word was barley released from his lips when she felt his dick pulsate inside her, liquid warmth flooding her pussy.

They collapsed on top of the smooth, polished wood, her head resting on his chest. Astrid inhaled the scent of sweat and their love-making. "Wow. I have to say that was the best sex I ever had. But, baby?"

"Yeah?" His voice vibrated against her ear.

"You're going to need a new table."

CHAPTER 21

Dannen screamed and banged on the wall of a forgotten house left to decay in an overgrown section of a subdivision. Dirt and debris crumbled leaving a dust cloud in its wake.

How had everything gone to shit so fast? She'd figured out who her traitors were from the beginning. They were no loss, they had the weakest powers. The others had powers that could've been gold to her. No matter. She still had enough Lespri allies to reach her goal.

Maybe it wasn't such a good idea, going after Richard's family. Her mother had been pathetic and weak. Looked down on, no more than an afterthought to the high-ranking Dreamers and the Legacy. She'd been ashamed to have her as a mother, but she *was* her blood. Maybe she deserved *some* justice. Her real target, and prize, was Astrid.

That sanctimonious bitch. She had some nerve. Treating her like a poor relative she had to take care of, pity. It was framed as her being a partner in the restaurants, but she knew deep inside, silent partner was what Astrid meant. Same shit, different circumstance.

Dannen paced the tiny room, trying to plan her next move. The Oracles would only give them another forty-eight hours. After that, they could no longer protect that bitch and her new-found allies. Right now, she could wait, bide her time. And when it comes, the chaos will be glorious.

***

"I think you heard what I said." Astrid pinned each member of the Legacy with a stern glance. "If the rest of you want to get out of this alive, you're going to have to work with me, and the Catchers."

A young blonde woman, who couldn't have been more than thirty, spoke up. "I am Rose, and it has been agreed that since the death of our *Lider*, I will speak for the Legacy." Although she had a heavy Russian accent, her English was flawless. "Are we all in one accord, ladies?" The nine young women surrounding her, various sizes, shades, and ethnicities, verbalized their consent, one by one, in the language of their homeland.

"Now, we have a few questions," Rose continued. "Since when are you working with the Catchers?"

Astrid studied Rose's face, along with the countenance of the other Legacy members. Hers was not a question, but an accusation. All of them saw her as a traitor. She decided the best answer was an honest one. They faced the same enemy. Trust had to start somewhere. "Since an undead Dreamer tried to kill me."

"We still don't believe this nonsense about Dannen," Rose scoffed. "The girl is dead. After your report, a fellow Dreamer identified her body for confirmation, and almost got captured for her trouble. There was a Catcher waiting at the morgue for her. We know the Catchers are responsible for all of this."

The other women of the Legacy nodded in agreement.

"The Catchers have come up with some pretty impressive ways to try and capture us." Rose's gaze settled on Lucien and Somiar, who flanked Astrid. "And using the mutts bred by Leila and her Catcher lover was a good one. But to create an enemy to both of us, so we can work together? I have to admit, *that* is genius. Maybe we should cut the crap and dispose of you now."

Lucien smirked. "You could try. This room is surrounded by Catcher stones. We deactivated them so you could get in. I'm sure you've noticed my ring." He raised his right hand, making sure his Catcher ring was at eye level for all to see.

Astrid fought to keep the surprise from her face. She hadn't noticed he wore his Catcher ring today. What was the deal with that? He was the only Catcher that seemed to not need it.

With a snap of his fingers, the ring glowed blood red. "The Catcher stones have been reactivated. None of you are going anywhere unless we let you. I suppose the 'mutts' aren't as stupid as you'd hoped."

"I knew it. I knew we couldn't trust you," Rose spat. She pulled a vial from her sleeve. "This contains a liquid that will evaporate when the glass breaks. The gas will join us back to our slumbering bodies, but kill everyone else in the room." An evil grin spread her lips. "We've been working on it for a while now. The only thorn in our sides was getting past the Catcher stones so we could make it into your house and use it. At last, we can say good-by to the abominations."

Before she could drop the fragile glass, it flew across the room into Astrid's grip. "Stop it!" Astrid's sharp tone surprised even her.

She'd never been so assertive in the presence of the Legacy. She was always so awestruck by their power and status, deference was her common position. But now, she saw them as they were. Human. Flawed. A bunch of power-hungry assholes.

She gave the vial to Somiar. "Take this. Have it analyzed. Make sure you use *all* our resources as a precaution."

"How did you do that?" Rose gasped.

Astrid thanked God she'd had the foresight to keep Kalyste hidden in the room. Her telekinesis came in handy. She knew the Legacy wouldn't trust them, and she had no idea what stunt they'd pull.

After Somiar's retreat, she returned her attention back to the Legacy. "Three members have already been killed. Do you really think we'd be here having this meeting if the Catchers were involved? They would continue exterminating you all like mice in a trap."

Lucien snapped his fingers. His ring stopped glowing. "The Catcher stones have been deactivated. Go ahead. Take your chances with that psycho. You're free to go."

Rose inclined her head, her countenance never changing. "Continue."

"I saw what Dannen did to them." Astrid looked at each of them. "If you're so all-powerful, why couldn't you stop them? Why did she succeed?"

When she got no response, she continued. "You don't know how to stop her, do you?'

Still no response from Rose or the Legacy.

"Here's the bottom line, ladies. You don't have to join us in this fight. We may lose. She'll take care of me, and your "abomination" problem." She wiggled her fingers in air quotes. "Then, she'll take care of you. *Her* abomination problem. She'll pick you off. Slowly. One by one. Savoring every moment of your demise. Almost climaxing in pleasure from your screams of agony. And then, when you're dead and gone, she'll turn the Dreamers and her new Legacy into something nightmares are made of."

Rose, a granite hard glare in her eyes spoke. "We will work with you." Without another word, the Legacy left the room, one by one.

"You think it was a good idea to let them go?" Lucien pulled Astrid into his embrace.

She rested her head on his chest and listened to his heartbeat, using it as sedative to ease her raw nerves and slow her own erratic rhythm. "There will be time for Dreamers and Catchers to hate each other again after we get rid of Dannen."

"What about us?" Lucien's question was almost a whisper.

"Good question." Astrid matched his tone. "I'll never see you as my enemy, but we haven't had time to be our drama-free selves. We'll find out what we are when the dust settles."

"Yeah," Lucien sighed. "Let's hope we aren't under the dirt."

Kalyste took corporeal form and joined the group. "I don't know what those women did to themselves, but I wasn't empathically aware of any of them. It was like they weren't in the room."

Lucien rubbed his chin. "You think it was because you were trying to use more than one power at the same time?"

"But I didn't. I wasn't using any of my other powers when I was trying to read them."

Astrid ran a hand through her hair. "We're trained at an early age to rein in our emotions. Legacy are masters at it."

Kalyste frowned, "I can read your emotions with no problem."

Astrid assumed a stoic expression. "Try it now."

Kalyste cocked her head. She stared at Astrid and her eyes widened. "I can still get a read, but it wasn't easy." She sidled closer to Astrid and whispered, "By the way, save the lust for after the fight."

"I will." Astrid giggled.

Lucien cleared his throat. "Excuse me, I'm still in the room. Didn't anyone ever tell you that whispering is rude?"

"Sorry." Astrid tried to keep the humor from her voice. It felt so good to have friendly banter again. So much of their lives had turned to shit.

She resumed a conversational tone. "Had I been Legacy, you wouldn't have been able to read me at all."

"Hmm." Kalyste nibbled her lip. "Good to know."

Lucien strolled to the water cooler near the stone stairs and poured a cup. "Where is this battle with Dannen supposed to happen?" He lounged against the wall, draining the cup with one long gulp.

"Well, the wedding invitations have the bottom of the Australian sea as the destination," Kalyste replied. Her casual tone was like she was talking about the weather.

Lucien stood ramrod straight. "Wedding?"

Astrid stared at Kalyste. "Come again?"

"Oh yeah. Didn't I mention you two are getting married?" Kalyste took a step back. "Um...I can read both of you now and I can tell you're anything but happy."

CHAPTER 22

"What the hell are you talking about?" Astrid glared at Kalyste trying to determine if she'd gone as crazy as Dannen. "We're not getting married."

"I'm afraid that was my idea." Richard's voice filled the room before he materialized.

Astrid stared him down. Never in her life had she wanted to punch him so badly. "Why the hell would you suggest something like that? And who the hell would attend an invitation at the bottom of the sea?"

Richard grinned. "Only people who could actually make it there. Let's say, the Legacy, certain Dreamers using their Dreamer bodies. And certain rogue Lespri."

"Rogues? I thought they were all taken care of by their soldiers." Astrid threw her hands up in resignation. "Don't tell me there are more."

Richard nodded. "Sorry to break it to you."

"Good grief," Astrid sighed. "Your people are so wishy washy." She palmed her forehead, trying to ward off a headache. "How are we supposed to know which Lespri ass to kick?"

"An Oracle from another Haven charmed the hearts of the guests. Friendly Lespri will have a yellow glow. Enemies will be red." Kalyste smiled.

Lucien's mouth gaped open. He must have realized how stupid he looked because shut it. "Another Haven? What do you mean another Haven? Yours isn't the only one? How many are there?"

Kalyste moistened her lips with the tip of her tongue. "That's not important. Just remember, red is bad. We've had them cover the Legacy and Dreamers with green."

Astrid wanted nothing more than for the past few days to be a distant memory. She knew what Kalyste was doing. This was a need-to-know case. "How does marriage come into play?"

"I counseled Dannen for several months and I know how her mind works." Richard shook his head. "You have no idea how much she absolutely hates you. As a matter of fact, she hates you more than she does me, and I killed her mother."

Astrid swallowed the lump in her throat. The fact that someone found her so contemptible, they were willing to throw immortality out the window didn't sit well. "I still don't understand any of this. I never did anything to her."

Lucien sat next to her on the couch. "It's not about that. Her problem isn't just with you. She hates herself, and anyone who reminds her she wasn't on their level." He moved closer to her. "You inadvertently made her feel less than enough, because she wasn't content with being the best version of herself. She wanted to be the best at everything."

He looked up at Richrd and winked. "The Catchers make us continue our education. Studying human behavior has become our thing." He took a deep breath. "But I still don't know where marriage comes in."

"It's how we flush her out and make her meet us on our terms. There's no way Dannen is going to let you have a happy day. She'll know that we'll be there, but because Kalyste is an Oracle, she can't join in the fighting. And I'm the only one with the capability to kill her."

Lucien rubbed the back of his neck. "I only hope the Legacy keeps their word and joins us. How much time do we have before the Oracles take matters into their own hands?"

"Two days." Kalyste nibbled her lip. "We've set the stage and a force field dome is in place. The Legacy will be sent coordinates so they can dream their way in. The wedding has also been leaked to the Lespri. Dannen's spies have surely told her about it by now."

Kalyste clasped her hands behind her and paced in front of Lucien and Astrid. "The cover story is that you are so madly in love, you wanted to get married before the final battle. Just in case one or both of you don't make it."

Astrid was sure her brows almost touched her hairline. "Dannen will never believe that. She may hate me, but she knows Dreamers don't think like that." She ignored Lucien's fidgeting next to her. She could feel his gaze on her as she spoke. It took everything in her not to look at him to gauge how her words affected him.

"We know there's a chance she won't buy it, but she still isn't going to let you have any type of happiness." Richard nodded. "She'll show up."

Lucien placed his hand in Astrid's.

Knowing it would be obvious she was trying to avoid looking at him after the gesture, she turned her face to is.

He caressed her fingers, an unsure smile playing at the corners of his lips. "Okay, baby. Time to save the world."

Chapter 23

Dannen wanted to dance in anticipation. Perched on the lip of a volcano in Hawaii, she gazed down into its molten depths. She was finally going to get what she wanted. Sure, it was a trap, but her end game was taking Astrid's life. Managing to survive long enough for the Oracle's to put an end to this miserable world would've been icing on the cake, but she could almost taste Astrid's blood in her mouth.

What pleased her most was how simple it was to get some of the Lespri on her side. They were so easy to manipulate. It helped that the Oracles were nothing but a bunch of sadists who got off on other people's misery.

She'd heard the story of Kalyste and Jude. The Oracles knew what he'd done to her, and still set him up as her counselor. She didn't know how Kalyste could forgive him.

And this shit with Cyrus? Why was she sent to the same Haven with that son of a bitch, and assigned her mother's killer as her counselor?

Fuck the Oracles. Fuck the Dreamers. Double fuck Astrid. Fuck the world.

Chapter 24

Astrid frowned at her image in the full body oval mirror. The jewel encrusted bodice of the white dress twinkled in the bright light. Crystals scattered over the flesh toned straps at her arms, elbows, and just above the sweetheart neckline gave the illusion of diamonds embedded in her skin. The white skirt billowed in sheer layers from her waist to the floor. Although the ballgown styled wedding dress was beautiful, it was one Astrid never would've chosen.

Unfortunately, it was needed for the coming battle. Her sword was hidden in the folds of the tear away skirt, daggers strapped to her legs. Throwing stars held her kinky coils in place at the top of her head.

Kalyste came up behind her, looking regal in a lavender silk halter dress. "I guess this is the closest I'll ever get to helping a daughter get ready for her wedding day."

"Don't get all sentimental on me," Astrid scoffed. "We both know what this is. Any minute now, all hell is going to break loose. Never thought I'd be wearing a wedding dress hiding an arsenal." She looked up at the colorful underwater wildlife swimming by. Coral and sea plants danced on the ocean floor. "Or getting married in a dome at the bottom of the sea."

The Lespri who were helping out, illuminated the world around them. It was pitch black outside the dome when they first arrived. Astrid didn't realize how dark it would be this far below the surface. With a shake of her head, she turned to face the woman she now considered a friend. "You and the other Lespri did a great job."

Somiar entered the room, her dress a shimmering swirl of silver silk. "Have you guys seen the rest of this place? It's magnificent."

Her eyes twinkled with a hint of mischief as she addressed Astrid. "You sure we can trust the Legacy? They've been chomping at the bit to get my brother and I together so they could kill us. Definitely not happy to see so many of them, or other Dreamers here."

Kalyste pressed her lips into a thin line. "We will not allow them pull any crap like that today. This is not the day to settle old scores."

Somiar plopped on the couch and studied the two women. "You both look beautiful." Nibbling her lip, she cocked her head. "You're giving off strong Cinderella vibes, Astrid."

"Yeah, I know. Definitely not my style, but hey, fake wedding, fake style." She threw a sidelong look to Kalyste. "Dannen and her crew will be here?"

"She will. Richard seems pretty sure of himself. I'm surprised she hasn't shown herself already." Kalyste went to sit next to Somiar. "Now remember, as an Oracle, I can't join in the fighting, but I've helped level the playing field. And although Richard is the only one who can kill her, ya'll can do some serious damage."

"Yeah, about that," Somiar interjected. "What are you going to do to us?"

"You mean what have I done. Your sleeping bodies are near Haven with the Oracles, and I've enhanced all of your powers. You all will be Dreamers and Catcher's on steroids. Whatever you could do before has been multiplied a hundredfold. Instant healing, enhanced strength, and speed. But you're not immortal. A fatal blow will still kill you."

Astrid swallowed the lump in her throat. "Give my thanks to the Lespri who came to help us out."

Kalyste gave a tight-lipped smile and smoothed her dress. "Ya'll ready?"

Astrid took a deep breath. "Guess so. Here comes the bride."

***

Lucien stood at the end of the aisle, waiting for the wedding to start. Malachi fidgeted next to him looking uncomfortable in a gray tux. He scanned the small number of guests, mostly strangers to him, all emitting an almost creepy green or yellow glow. The only familiar Lespri faces were Jude and his dad.

His mom, was shooting daggers at him with her glare. She'd been ready to box his ears when she was told she and Stephen's memories had been erased so they wouldn't interfere with this fight.

Had it not been for Kalyste insisting she be there to make the wedding look authentic, she still wouldn't be involved. He'd heard ad-nauseum how it was a mother's duty to protect her child. Apparently, she hadn't gotten the memo that he was a grown ass man.

Stephen sat next to her, patting her hand.

Lucien made sure they were seated far from Richard. He could tell his dad still felt a certain type of way about their relationship.

He ignored the hostile looks from the Legacy.

The Atrium was bright, the dome shining in the artificial light supplied by the Lespri. The view outside the dome reminded him of the underwater rooms at the aquarium in downtown Atlanta. Orchids and lilies covered the columns and chairs, so many, it was almost garish.

"Afraid I'm to blame for the flowers. I thought Astrid might like them. Besides, a friend said they're going to be really helpful later." The soft feminine voice in his head made him take a step back.

He almost bumped into Malachi. "Did you hear that?"

"What? I didn't hear anything," Malachi said with a frown. "You okay?"

Lucien nodded. "Yeah, must be nerves."

"You're not hearing things. I'm the blonde in the front, with the daisies in her hair."

Lucien gazed at the petite, blonde, white woman discreetly waving.

"Sorry we didn't get to meet. I'm Ella, and this is my husband, Blake." With a friendly smile, she motioned to the black man next to her. He was an almost freakishly muscle-bound man whose height dwarfed her. *"We're here to help."*

He could hear her plain as day, but her lips weren't moving. There was something familiar about her voice. Lucien inclined his head in gratitude, and mouthed a thank you, still trying to wrap his brain around the strange powers of the Lespri.

The string quartet in the corner began to play. Lucian's gaze was riveted on the silver doors slowly opening at the other end of the cavernous room.

Somiar glided down the aisle and took her place in front of the flower covered arch, followed by Kalyste.

The orchestra began the wedding march and the guests all stood and faced the back of the hall, waiting for the bride.

Lucien couldn't stop his wide grin when Astrid appeared at the entrance. She was stunning. An angelic smile on her face, she took small steps toward him. They locked gazes, transfixed. He knew this wedding was a sham but found himself at odds with his feelings. *If only.* He refused to let himself finish the thought.

Forcing his mind to focus, he broke her gaze to survey their surroundings. His body tingled.

As he watched her descend down the aisle, everything went hazy.

The scenery in the room changed. He was back at his house, on the terrace having breakfast. Astrid joined him and planted a kiss on his neck. He pulled her onto his lap and placed his lips to hers.

In a blink, he was back under the dome, Astrid continuing to make her way to his side. She stood next to him, then leaned in to lightly place her lips on his.

Something wasn't right. Her kiss was different. A sharp pain ripped through his abdomen. Looking down at her hands, he saw the dagger in her grip. The blood that coated his hands vanished, and the abdominal wound healed.

"It's Dannen!" Leila screamed.

Richard charged her, but she disappeared.

Dannen appeared at the entrance, dressed in Astrid's wedding gown. She ran down the aisle at full speed. "Baby, are you okay?"

Lucien swung with all his might, punching her in the face, knocking her off her balance. "If you've hurt her, I'll kill you." He grabbed her around the throat, and yanked her to her feet. "Where is she!"

Dannen's eyes widened. "Lucien, what's the matter with you? It's me. Astrid."

Lucien clenched his jaw. This bitch really was crazy. His heart hammered. What if he was too late? He flung Dannen away from him.

Richard had his sword raised to finish her. Lucien grabbed his arm. "Wait. We have to find out what she did to Astrid."

"Lucien," Dannen sobbed. "What's wrong with you? What's wrong with all of you? I'm Astrid."

He stared down at her and met her gaze. Although he still saw Dannen's face, her confused and loving gaze told him not to believe his eyes. "Oh shit!" He kneeled next to her, caution mixed with hope. Slowly, he brought his lips to hers.

Yes. This was her kiss, the kiss he knew so well.

Dannen's face disappeared and Astrid was left in her place.

"Oh, God Astrid, I'm so sorry. I didn't know it was you. I'd never..." Before he could finish the sentence, chaos erupted.

***

Several women, different sizes and shapes burst into the room screaming like banshees. A shimmering red glow outlined their bodies. Astrid stared in horror as two Dreamers were attacked from behind, their throats slit so deep, their heads were almost severed.

Kalyste waved her hands and all the chairs in the room disappeared, giving them a clear space to fight.

Astrid leaped to her feet and ripped the bottom of her dress away transforming into her Dreamer garb, as did all the Legacy and the remaining Dreamers.

The traitor Lespri heading in her direction, changed course and attacked the other occupants in the room. Full-fledged fighting ensued, but no one engaged Astrid.

Lucien grimaced. "I think Dannen has put everyone on notice to leave you to her."

Astrid nodded. They turned when they heard Ella shriek.

An invisible force attacked her, cuts and bruises appearing, then disappearing as she healed. She wildly swung her long sai, hoping to hit her assailant with a lucky jab. Her husband attempted to help her in the fight, but how do you fight what you can't see?

"We've got to help them." Lucien ran over to help, but had as little success as the other two. He got several wounds for his trouble, some way too close to fatal for comfort.

Astrid sprinted in his direction and was thrown back by and invisible force. "Okay, I'm sick of this see-through bitch."

There was one way to get rid of her. That freaky thing he did where he could see through another's eyes. He needed to use their attacker's eyes. She needed to get close enough to Lucien to tell him her plan.

He said that only works with his sister.

Astrid whirled around. Several Lespri and Dreamers were still engaged in the fight. "Who said that?"

It's Ella. Telepath. He said that only works with his sister.

His powers have been enhanced. If he can see through invisible girl's eyes, he can tell you where she is. It'll also render her blind. I'll cover you while he does his thing.

Apparently, Lucien got the message. He backed against the wall and his eyes went black.

Astrid intercepted a Lespri woman charging at Lucien and ran her through with her sword. The woman grinned, pushing the sword from her body, knocking Astrid off balance.

She flipped back and regained her footing.

The woman's wound immediately healed. Shit. She forgot the only way to kill these demon bitches was to sever their heads.

Pulling one of the stars from her hair, Astrid threw it at her opponent, the sharp metal meeting its mark, embedded in her eye.

With a grin, the woman ripped it out, healing again. "I don't care what Dannen said, you're mine." She went on all fours and transformed into a cheetah. With a roar, it sprang at Astrid, teeth bared and dripping with saliva.

Astrid raised an arm, knowing the defensive move wouldn't save her from becoming dinner.

While the animal was in mid-air, its head and body went in two separate directions, leaving Astrid splattered in blood.

Nicolette, clad head to toe in a black leather catsuit, stood over Astrid, and flashed a smile. "Always knew that trick bitch was into cannibalism." Not giving Astrid a chance to reply, she went to pulling flowers from the vines on the walls, throwing them at several Lespri enemies. The flowers spun like the wheels of a circular saw, becoming pretty, but deadly weapons slicing through flesh and bone.

Astrid attempted to follow suit, but the flowers wouldn't budge from their position.

"Sorry, chicky." Nicolette chuckled. "These only work for me. You're going to have to use your own tools to save your ass." Nicolette sprinted across the room, throwing the lethal blooms ahead of her, taking out several screaming women.

"I make a perfect tool." Leila's voice came from over Astrid's shoulder.

Astrid turned to see Lucien's mother standing behind her, rivulets of blood decorating her black leather catsuit. "I bet you do. Don't ever want to be on your bad side."

"Do right by my son, that won't be an issue."

"No problem. Duck."

Leila didn't hesitate to squat down low to the floor as Astrid rammed her sword over Leila's head, shoving it into the eye of the Lespri behind Leila.

Jude finished the woman off with the swing of his blade, then disappeared.

Astrid twisted her lips. "Is it a bad thing that I'm getting used to heads flying?"

A sardonic smile crept to Leila's face. "Welcome to being the new miss bad- ass." She pulled Astrid into a crushing embrace.

***

Lucien used the Lespri's disorientation to his advantage. As long as he controlled her vision, he could see, but she couldn't. Not wanting to tip off what he was doing, he spoke to Ella with his mind.

Turn around, Ella, and telepathically tell your husband to stand down.

When he could see her face, he continued his instructions. *Step back three paces. Raise your sai a little higher.*

Ella did as she was told.

Let your husband know that when you swing, he needs to swing right after you at shoulder level."

He saw Ella nod through his captor's eyes. *Swing now!*

Ella's sai hummed as it sliced through the air and met with the muscle and bone of the Lespri's mid-section.

Immediately following, Blake's sword was no more than a blur as it came toward the Lespri's neck.

Lucien released himself from his enemy's vision in time for her to see her own demise.

Her corpse materialized at their feet, blood streaming from her headless body forming a red pool against the stark white marble floor.

Blake stepped over the body as if she were no more than a small log in his way and rushed to hug his wife. "I am in your debt, sir."

Lucien was briefly surprised by the burly man's British accent.

"I owe you for saving my wife's life. Now let's go save yours."

Lucien didn't bother to correct him. All he wanted was for it to be true. Leave it to him to realize he loved someone when there was a chance he could lose her. Right now, that wasn't an option. "I lost sight of her while using the Lespri's vision. No telling where she is now."

Blake nodded. "We'll split up." The Threesome all went in opposite directions,

He scanned the room for Astrid, his desperation growing with each passing second.

Noticing a Lespri traitor getting the drop on a Dreamer, Lucien stopped his search to take over the enemy Lespri's eyesight, giving the Dreamer an advantage.

The Dreamers were surprisingly good team fighters, considering they'd always worked alone.

A Dreamer or two would engage a Lespri for long enough for a Lespri ally to do the decapitation. They'd decimated most of the traitors, and it was clear their enemy was fighting a losing battle.

He spotted Astrid in the center of the room, swords clashing with a Lespri woman. Her sword met its mark with the woman's throat, leaving her head attached by a thin strip of muscle. A Lespri soldier appeared behind her and finished the job.

When their gazes locked, she ran to him, smiling.

Dannen materialized in front of one of the columns, an evil smile distorting her otherwise beautiful features. In her grip was a gold sledgehammer. She twisted her body and swung the tool, striking the concrete with enough force for it to crumble.

"Astrid!" Lucien shouted.

Too late, Astrid looked up and saw the debris crashing toward her, knocking her over. The heavy stone covered her legs, rendering her immobile.

Lucien knew Dannen's plan. As long as Astrid was pinned, she wouldn't be able to heal. It was the same tactic Monica used on Somiar years ago.

He raced across the room but was no match for Dannen's ability to instantaneously materialize.

Dannen kneeled at Astrid's side, her knee planted on Astrid's hand. The tip of her dagger poised over Astrid's heart. Her words were almost a cackle as she stared emotionlessly at her rival, then back at Lucien. "All of you are such fools. Did you really think I gave a damn about winning against any of you? I knew this was a losing battle. None of you are important to me." She grinned evilly at Astrid. "Except you."

Lespri soldiers appeared behind their traitorous charges, awaiting Ella's judgement.

The remnant of Lespri traitors all spoke at once. Fragmented sentences, some louder than others.

"Forgive!"

"We didn't know!"

"She tricked us!"

"Mercy!"

Ella stood before the condemned. "For breaking our sacred laws. Harm no human, kill no Lespri. You have all been found guilty. The sentence is death."

The soldier's decapitated their charges with one blow of the sword.

Ella turned her attention to Dannen, still poised with her blade at Astrid's unconscious body. "That includes you."

Richard appeared behind Dannen and raised his sword. She pressed the tip of her blade into Astrid's flesh, drawing blood. "You can't kill me before I finish her."

"Dad no!" Lucien yelled.

Dannen glared at the surviving Dreamers and Legacy. "The end of the Legacy would have been icing on the cake." She looked down at Astrid. "But this was all about you, princess. I'll go to hell happy knowing I'm taking you with me."

"Don't do this." Lucien took over Dannen's vision, hoping the disorientation would give him a chance to save Astrid.

"I'm sorry, son." Richard's voice was almost a whisper. "We can't save her."

With a sigh that almost sounded orgasmic, Dannen rammed the blade deep into Astrid's chest and twisted it, widening the wound, but not removing the blade. Blood gushed from Astrid's chest.

Lucien wrenched himself from Dannen's eyes, not wanting to give her the satisfaction of watching Astrid die, but knowing he couldn't handle the sight himself. He reclaimed his own eyesight, to see shock and disbelief replace Dannen's evil countenance.

"No, it can't be," Dannen screeched. "No!"

He watched, detached and emotionless, as Richard took Dannen's head.

Forcing himself from his catatonic state, he forced his feet to move. Tears coursed down his cheeks, blurring his vision. Lucien made his way to Astrid's body. His heart caught in his throat when he stared into his mother's lifeless eyes.

His mind could not connect to what he saw. Glaring up at his father's astonished face, he willed his voice to work. "What the hell is this?

Somiar darted across the room, Malachi hot on her heels. "No!" She fell to her knees next to her mother, blood from the floor soaking into the knees of her black pants. "No, no, no!" Her blood-streaked face mixed with tears. "Mom," she wailed.

Malachi pulled Somiar into his embrace, holding her tight, a gentle palm running up and down her spine.

The Lespri dematerialized from the room.

Dreamers and Legacy surrounded the family. The Italian lilt of a Legacy member broke the silence. "There has been much bloodshed here today. We have lost many of our sisters to rid ourselves of a common enemy. We will give you time to mourn your mother."

Lucien glared at the face of his enemy. Although she wore her young façade, there was something tired and old in her face.

She continued, "This we do out of respect for our brief alliance. But make no mistake, you are still our enemy."

Without another word, the Dreamers and Legacy disappeared from the room.

Lucien pressed his lips together, disgusted at the words from the Legacy. After all this shit. They still couldn't come together. How many more would have to die?

He gazed up at his father. "Where's Astrid?" He choked the words out on a strangled breath. "If she's not here, where is she?"

Richard shook his head. "I don't know. I swear I don't."

Lucien motioned Kalyste to his side, and pushed at the concrete trapping Leila's legs. "Can you get this off her?"

Kalyste dropped to her knees next to him and stared down at the dead woman. "Y-yes. Of course," she stammered. She raised her shaking hands, palms up, over the rubble until the heavy column levitated high enough for Lucien to pull Leila free.

Stephen staggered into the room, blood trickling from a deep gash at his temple. "What happened?"

His gaze trailed to Lucien. "Oh, God. Leila!" He knelt next to Lucien and took his love into his arms rocking her. "Come on baby." He kissed her cheek. "Breathe." He sobbed, his chest heaving. "You can't do this to me." He wailed so loudly, Lucien's heart broke all over again.

Lucien grabbed Stephen's shoulders, gently shaking him. "Stephen, listen to me. Have you seen Astrid? We can't find her. Have you seen her?"

Stephen gazed blankly at him and shook his head. "No," he whispered. "I haven't."

Somiar, spent from her sobs, turned in her husband's arms and a gasped for air. "The last time I saw her, she was helping Leila fight one of the Lespri traitors. Jude ended the traitor."

Blake stepped forward. "I can tell you how Leila ended up here, but I don't know where she left Astrid."

"What do you mean?" Lucien rose, knowing this huge dude could knock him on his ass with one punch. But he was willing to risk it if it meant finding Astrid alive.

"I made a vow to you when you saved my wife, that I would save yours. Leila asked if I could find a Lespri who could make her look like your Astrid. Said she was told on 'good authority,'" he made air quotes with his fingers, "that it was the only way to save Astrid and end Dannen."

At Kalyste's audible gasp, Lucien turned to her, his expression grim. "Spill it, Kalyste. What do you know?"

"I was just thinking...that...if you um..." she hesitated.

Lucien glared at her. "You know something, and if you do, you'd better tell me right now or so help me..."

Jude stepped up and stood in front of his wife, hell in his eyes. "Someone better help you, because if you even think about threatening my wife again, I'll rip out your tongue."

"Both of you just cut it out!" Kalyste shouted. She came between the two men and faced her husband. "It's ok, baby." Placing her palms on both sides of his face, she gave him a gentle kiss on the lips. "I know you got my back, but I got this."

He smiled down at her, and with a slight nod, stepped away.

Turning back to face Lucien, she pursed her lips. "What I was about to suggest, is that you use Astrid's eyes to find her. Your power is still magnified, but I can only justify it for another few minutes. Now that the fight is over, I have to change all of your powers back to their original strength."

Without hesitation, Lucien's eyes went black. "It's dark. She must be unconscious."

"Control her eyes," Kalyste coached. "Open them."

He strained to do as he was told. "She's on a bed. White walls. There's a window."

"Is there any color at all?"

"No, none. Just white everywhere." Lucien blinked, his eyes returning to their normal light brown color. "That's all I saw."

Kalyste sighed. "I know where she is. She's returned to her body. She's not dreaming right now. Her body isn't here."

"I don't understand."

"She's at Haven." Kalyste's brows drew together. "I don't get why she's rejoined her body. Wouldn't she have to be pinned for that to happen?"

Lucien, glanced down at Stephen, still cradling Leila's body. "Stephen, do you have your Dreamer pin on you?"

Stephen shook his head. "No. I thought I lost it during the fight." Understanding overcame his features. "Leila took it, didn't she?" Fresh tears streamed down his cheeks. "She took it and pinned Astrid, then knocked me out."

"We need to get back to the house," Somiar said. Her eyes were red and puffy, her voice wobbled as if she were trying to choke back another round of tears. "I can't take being here anymore. Kalyste, if you would return our bodies back to our house." She embraced her husband. "I'll dream us back."

Kalyste inclined her head. "I'll take care of it."

CHAPTER 25

"Dad, you need to start from the beginning." Lucien poured a shot of whiskey from the bar, his hands still shaky from the loss of his mother. His mind was a jumble, so many pieces to unravel and fit together.

Since he, Somiar, and Leila had all been reunited, he thought the family drama was over. Sure, they still had to deal with the Dreamers and Legacy, but he thought secrets were a thing of the past.

Astrid accepted the crystal glass offered to her. "I don't understand why Leila would pin me."

Richard sighed. "She was trying to keep you safe. I know Leila can be a loose cannon, but I've never known her to be delusional. She said Dannen would die and you," he gestured to Lucien, "would be the key, and everything would work out the way it was supposed to. Then she jumped back into the fight."

"But how could she know that? How could she know any of it?" Lucien poured himself a shot and downed it in one gulp. The drink burned its way down his throat, but did nothing to soothe his raw nerves.

"I don't know, son. I asked Kalyste if one of the Lespri could have told her, but she said no. The only Lespri soldiers allowed to fight were the ones who had rogues in the battle. And none of them could see the future. Pretty good thing too. Knowing the future can have some pretty damnable outcomes."

"Where is Kalyste anyway?" Lucien looked around the room.

"You won't see her again. Or any of the Lespri. After she wiped the Dreamers and the Legacy's memories of us, her job was done. As far as they know, their members were killed in freak accidents and the Dreamers who lost their lives did so on assignment."

"Hard to believe they'd fall for the part about the Legacy," Astrid said.

"They have no choice. There's no other evidence, but they have beefed up their security and precautions. Unfortunately, they suspect the Catchers. We couldn't think of another way."

"Are you going to wipe our minds too?" Lucien looked crestfallen. "I don't' want to lose you again."

"No, the Lespri trust you, but I have to go. I was hoping to see Somiar before I left."

"Sorry, dad. I don't' think she's ready."

"Let me speak for myself little brother." Somiar strolled into the room from the direction of the kitchen. "I wasn't going to come. Malachi convinced me I'd hate myself if I missed this chance."

Richard's eyes shone with unshed tears. "I wish I could have spent more time with my son-in-law. And I wish with all my heart I had more time with you. Your brother had time with me before my death. You never got that. I'm so sorry."

Somiar crossed the room and embraced him. "It's okay, daddy. It wasn't your fault."

Astrid downed the rest of her glass and stood. "I'll give you all some privacy. I need to go get my things together anyway." She climbed the stairs slowly, looking like she'd lost her best friend.

Tears ran unchecked down Richard's cheeks. "Didn't know that one word would turn me into a blubbering idiot." He pulled back to take in his daughter. "I'm so proud of you." He kept one arm around her and held the other out to his son.

Lucien joined them for a group hug.

"I'm so proud of both of you." He stepped back and started to fade. Before he disappeared from sight, he smiled at Lucien. "Be sure Astrid is at Leila's funeral. Congratulations, son. You had two visions of your soul mate." Then he was gone.

***

Astrid stood in the center of the room she had occupied for the last week, and realized she had nothing to pack. Nothing belonged to her. All she had to do now was follow Richard's lead and say good-bye.

Forcing herself not to do the cowardly thing and pull an Irish exit, she waited, trying to make sure she gave enough time for Lucien and his family to say their goodbyes.

She didn't expect it to be so hard to leave this place. She'd come to love the sense of belonging his family provided. If she were honest, she loved the man who owned this house.

But he'd never said anything about loving her. They'd made no commitments. He didn't owe her a thing.

Fuck! What a time to let her guard down. Decades spent learning to rein in her emotions, and she was almost ready to toss it all to hell and tell him how she felt and let the chips fall where they may. Almost. What a big word with such few letters.

Afraid she would lose her nerve, she straightened her shoulders. Her hand gripped the doorknob. Time to say good-bye to the man she loved. She jumped back when the door opened, Lucien framed in the doorway.

"Oh, good. You haven't left yet." He swept past her and sat on the couch, patting the cushion next to him. "Come sit with me."

Unable to trust herself to speak, she took a seat, willing her hands not to tremble when he took them in his.

When he didn't say anything, she gazed up at him, trying to get a read. "I'm so sorry about your mom."

His lips tightened into a thin line. "Yeah, me too. Somiar and I are getting together day after tomorrow to make the arrangements. Only immediate family."

"Got it. I would still like to send flowers. Just let me know where to send them."

Lucien cocked his head. "You're not coming?"

Astrid licked her dry lips. "You said immediate family."

Unable to take the silence anymore, she extricated her hands. "I've got to go. I've spent too much time away from my restaurants and I need to make sure everything's alright."

She laughed nervously. "My assistant was ready to call the police when I talked to her yesterday. Besides, I want to make sure she didn't do anything weird, like put octopus eggs on the menu." She rubbed her sweaty palms on her pants. "Do octopus lay eggs?"

Realizing she was rambling, she stood on rubbery legs, and made her way to the door.

"Astrid! I want you to be immediate family." He almost shouted the words.

Her feet felt like she had magnets attached to them. After several seconds, she regained her composure and faced him. "I don't understand."

"Come back to me." He opened his arms to her.

Forcing her feet to move, she crossed the room, sidestepping his offer of an embrace. "What's going on, Lucien?"

"I love you, Astrid. I should have told you that a long time ago."

Her heart pounded in her ears. No sure she heard him right, she stepped closer to him, her body barely touching his. She gazed into his eyes. "Say it again."

"I love you." He kissed her lips.

"I love you." His breath caressed her cheek.

"I love you." He cupped the back of her head.

"And I love you." She offered her lips up to him, savoring the tingle throughout her body.

"You know, when I said I wanted you to be immediate family, I meant for life." He kissed her forehead and smiled. "Will you marry me?"

"Yes, Lucien. I will marry you. I'm yours." She reveled in his embrace. "Forever."

EPILOGUE

Kalyste paced the meeting chamber of the Oracles, trying to keep an open mind about what she knew one of them had done. She nibbled on her top lip as she watched her kin file into the room and take their seats at the black onyx table dominating the room.

Clodio, the oldest Lespri and the ancestor of all the Oracles present spoke first. "You're troubled my daughter?"

No matter how much Kalyste heard Clodio refer to her as "daughter" it made her want to laugh. Although she knew he had to be at least twenty-five when he died in order to be a Lepri, he looked like a teenager. Oh, the perks of living before the year 1300. No pollution, no global warming. You had to get out and hunt to get your food. Kept him in great physical shape.

But he wasn't the Oracle she was interested in at the moment. "Alizan." Kalyste pinned the named Oracle with her gaze. "What have you done?"

Alizan narrowed her eyes and stood, leaning forward, her palms resting on the table. "All here know what I have done. Except you. You are a young one."

Kalyste spoke through clenched teeth. "My age as an Oracle has nothing to do with what happened to Leila. Lespri with the gift of sight were forbidden to interfere with the fight."

"I don't have the gift of sight. Exactly. The gift of probability is different. I saw all the probable outcomes, and presented them to Leila. She could have chosen to sacrifice herself, her children, or both. She made her choice."

"That's splitting hairs and you know it." This was the first time Kalyste ever wanted to stamp her foot. "We weren't supposed to interfere in the fight."

"I interfered no more than you did, sister." Alizan cast a humorless smile, and tossed her raven-black hair over her shoulder. "You enhanced their power."

"But my actions were sanctioned by all the Oracles." Kalyste had to fight to keep her composure.

"So was Alizan's." Clodio went to stand next to Kalyste. "We did what we had to do to make sure Dannen didn't survive, my daughter. We didn't think one as young as you would understand our decision."

Not knowing if she were ready for the answer, Kalyste asked anyway. "What decision?"

"What should happen if another Dreamer becomes Lespri?"

Kalyste swallowed the lump in her throat. "And the answer?"

Clodio's eyes were sharp as daggers. "Instant final death."

ALSO BY SHAWN DALTON-SMITH

Dreamers

Life After

Ella Ever After

www.ingramcontent.com/pod-product-compliance
Lightning Source LLC
Chambersburg PA
CBHW030855200726
48289CB00003B/758